SON OF THE SIOUX

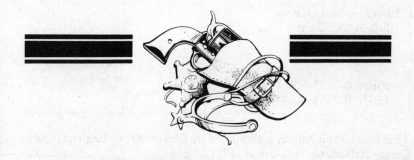

Gerald Drayson Adams

ATLANTIC LARGE PRINT
Chivers Press, Bath, England.
Curley Publishing, Inc.,
South Yarmouth, Mass., USA.

Library of Congress Cataloging-in-Publication Data

Adams, Gerald Drayson.
  Son of the Sioux / Gerald Drayson Adams.
    p. cm.—(Atlantic large print)
  ISBN 0–7927–0550–5 (softcover)
[PR9619.3.A32S66 1991]
823—dc20   90–19819
                                   CIP

British Library Cataloguing in Publication Data

Adams, Gerald Drayson
  Son of the Sioux.
  I. Title
  823.914 [F]

  ISBN 0–7451–8066–3
  ISBN 0–7451–8078–7 pbk

This Large Print edition is published by Chivers Press, England, and Curley Publishing, Inc, U.S.A. 1991

Published by arrangement with Dorchester Publishing Company, Inc.

U.K. Hardback ISBN 0 7451 8066 3
U.K. Softback ISBN 0 7451 8078 7
U.S.A. Softback ISBN 0 7927 0550 5

AUTHOR'S NOTE

This novel is a work of fiction, but the main characters and events herein are based on historical facts.

Among the real-life events are the Grattan Massacre, the Sand Creek Massacre, and the Platte River Crossing Fight. Such places as Fort Laramie and Fort Lyon are also actual places.

Many of the persons who appear in this book have left their mark on the pages of history. Historical characters include Lt. Caspar Collins and Major Rufus Collins, Jim Bridger (known as 'Big Throat' among the Indians), Crazy Horse, Little Big Man, and other Sioux and Cheyenne chiefs.

CHAPTER ONE

The dark curtain of rain swept westward as thunder grumbled in the distance. Overhead the morning sun broke through and a rainbow hung across the sky, vanishing behind the towering ramparts of Crow Butte. The air felt clean and damp from the heavy downpour.

A six wagon Army supply column appeared through a gap in the hills, following a faint trail over the short buffalo grass on the down slope. The supply column was escorted by a detail of twelve troopers and a sergeant. Riding in advance was Jim Bridger, Indian scout under contract to the Third Cavalry at Fort Laramie. His smoke-blackened buckskins were in sharp contrast to his alert blue eyes, made more striking by a four-day growth of whiskers. Jim Bridger was noted among the whites for his caustic sense of humor and among the Indians for an enlarged goiter, earning him the name of Big Throat.

Riding the hard seat of the lead wagon beside the driver was Second Lieutenant Caspar Collins, aged twenty-two, gray-eyed, black-haired, slim-waisted and six-feet-one of bone and sinew. Caspar had placed number seven in the graduating class of 1864 at West Point Military Academy. Upon receiving their commissions, these neophytes were granted a two-week furlough, which was usually spent either on a honeymoon, visiting their fiancées or on a glorious bender among the fleshpots of New York City. After this short-lived freedom they would report to the various regiments of their choice, hoping for quick battlefield promotion in the war against the Confederacy.

Caspar had indulged in none of these time honored customs. Instead he had taken a deferred graduation furlough and had headed west on a supply train bound for the post of his choice on the Indian Frontier at Fort Laramie, Wyoming Territory.

The driver of the lead wagon was Private Turk, a sour dispositioned young man of twenty-five, who chewed angrily on his tobacco plug and occasionally cast side glances at this brand new second lieutenant beside him who discouraged all attempts at prolonged conversation. In the book of the loquacious Private Turk, this made him just another rank-happy, West Point bastard. To this he added the lieutenant probably had a yellow streak and had chosen the Indian Frontier to escape action against the Confederate armies. In making this momentous deduction, Private Turk chose not to remember that when he was drafted he headed west at his own expense and enlisted in Quartermaster Corps at Fort Union to escape getting his head blown off by a Confederate cannonball. As the supply columns were usually well guarded, the chances were remote that he would lose his red hair to some scalp-hungry Sioux or Cheyenne.

Meanwhile Caspar, unaware of Private Turk's growing antagonism, was completely preoccupied recognizing old familiar landmarks: towering Crow Butte and the rolling slopes and gullies covered with buffalo grass where he had spent many happy boyhood days riding and hunting with his close Indian friends of the Oglala tribe of the Lakota Nation. He remembered Tashunka, the quiet young son of Crazy Horse, the Oglala holy man; He Dog, who loved nothing better than a practical joke; Lone Bear, the son of Man Afraid; and Little Singing Stream, the pretty eight-year-old daughter of Chief Spotted Tail who could race her pinto pony with the best of them.

The distant dark rain curtain moved further to the west and sunlight gleamed on the water at a bend in the Shell River, where ten years before the lodges of the Oglala and Brule Lakotas had camped, waiting for the Indian agent to distribute the good blankets, molasses, sugar and tobacco sent by the Indian Bureau in Washington.

At first light when young Caspar, aged twelve, left Fort Laramie on his buckskin pony, a birthday gift from his father, to go on a secret hunt with his friends Tashunka and Little Singing Stream, he had no premonition that the day would end in torn friendships, blood, and death.

Caspar, Tashunka and Little Singing Stream stole out of the Oglala camp, forded the Shell River and, breaking out of the low hanging mist into bright sunlight, put their ponies to a lope pointed toward the vastness of Crow Butte. The previous evening they had sighted a small herd of buffalo moving into a wooded gully. Among the herd was a white buffalo, whose hide would be a most-prized possession to any Lakota.

White buffalo were scarce. Only seven had been seen in the last decade, and the boys were determined to bring back the hide of this white buffalo, a big thing to show among the great lodge circles of the Lakotas.

Caspar wore fringed buckskins and a weatherbeaten campaign hat, the front brim turned up and riveted to the crown with the brass badge of the Third Cavalry. He was armed with a breechloading Sharp's carbine and a hunting knife at his belt. Tashunka, slim, wiry, light-skinned with light-brown hair—unusual for a Lakota—worn in a single brain, a bearclaw necklace on his bare chest, a deerskin breechclout and moccasins, was armed with a short buffalo bow, a quiver of arrows and a hunting knife. Little Singing

Stream tagged behind the boys on her pinto pony, expertly leading a pack pony by a rawhide thong. Her heart-shaped, delicately featured face was framed by a wealth of blue-black hair worn in two braids bound up with beaver fur. Her eyes dark brown, rather than the usual Lakota black, were thickly limned with blue-black lashes, and her soft doeskin smock, leggings and small moccasins were intricately decorated with porcupine quills and colorful beadwork.

Dropping down into a draw they found the herd of buffalo and the white buffalo, a bull calf. Tashunka, who wanted to be the one to kill it, yelled the Lakota war cry, '*Hokahey! Hokahey!*' and charged, plying his wrist whip. Caspar was right at his heels, equally anxious to be the one to make the kill.

The buffalo stampeded. Tashunka closed in on the white buffalo, notched an arrow to his bowstring and, just as he shot, the buffalo swerved and the arrow struck its shaggy mane. Before he could notch another arrow Caspar cut in, raced alongside the bull, and sent the heavy bullet from the Sharp's carbine crashing into the great head, just behind the ear, dropping the animal in its tracks. While the rest of the herd thundered away in a cloud of dust, Caspar and Tashunka, whooping with delight, leapt from their ponies, whipping out their hunting knives to skin the prized trophy.

5

In the Brule encampment, though the smoke rose lazily from the cookfires giving forth the aspect of peace, there was trouble brewing, big trouble. The great lodge circle was deserted. Women and children were scurrying for the cover of the canebreaks in the river bottoms. They were followed by hundreds of warriors, their hands full of weapons. Caspar, Tashunka and Little Singing Stream raced into camp, plying their wrist whips and whooping loudly.

The big sounds died in their throats and they drew rein in quick alarm, for coming at a gallop from the Oglala encampment was a lieutenant with an Iowa scout called Wyuse, followed by a wagonload of infantry and two caissons towing two howitzer field guns.

'They promised us sugar, coffee, flour, molasses and good blankets,' Tashunka spat angrily. 'Instead they send Soldier Coats and wagon-guns! Why is this, Cas?'

'Must be on account of that mangy Mormon cow the Brules killed yesterday, the one that was crazed on loco weed.' Caspar made tight-lipped reply. 'Anyway, it spells trouble because the young Soldier Coat Chief is Lieutenant Grattan, who never passes up a chance to shoot Indians.'

'And with him is that drunken Wyuse whose mouth is always full of bad words for the Lakotas!'

From a low ridge behind the lodges they

6

watched the soldiers gallop into the great lodge circle, where the lieutenant bawled orders and the infantry leapt down from the wagons and formed up, rifles at the ready. The gun crews unlimbered. The gun pointers aimed the field guns at the lodges while the crews loaded. Lieutenant Grattan and Wyuse walked their horses forward as tall, dignified Chief Conquering Bear and his brother Little Thunder came from the main lodge to meet them. Wyuse's red eyes squinted around the deserted lodge circle.

Wyuse spoke in a voice from the side of his mouth. 'Lieutenant, when you don't see no squaws, no kids and no warriors, them Lakotas is up to somethin'. Better git back to yer guns and be ready to crack into 'em!'

Lieutenant Grattan wheeled his horse and loped back to his guns. Wyuse spat out his chaw of tobacco, pulled a bottle from his pocket and took a deep swallow, wiped his mouth on his sleeve and drew rein in front of Chief Conquering Bear and Little Thunder.

'Hear me, Conquering Bear,' he snarled. 'Yesterday a white man's cow was killed among your lodges. The Soldier Coats have come for the gawdam Injun what done it!'

'The Indian you seek is a Minneconjou. He is a guest in my lodge and is therefore under my protection,' Conquering Bear replied with quiet dignity. 'This matter can be settled with good heart. Conquering Bear will pay the

7

white man one mule and five fine horses. But the cow was mad. It had knocked down two of our lodges. It had to be killed!'

'The Soldier Coats don't want yer fuckin' horses! Hand over that Injun or the wagon-guns'll knock down more of yer stinkin lodges!'

Conquering Bear's face filled with anger, but before he could speak, a handsome young warrior stepped out of Conquering Bear's lodge, an arrow notched to his bowstring and resolutely faced Wyuse.

'Straight Foretop killed the mad cow!' he stated.

'Drop yer weapons and march over to the Soldier Coats! An' do it on the double!'

Straight Foretop's hand tightened on his bow, his voice was strong and clear. 'The whites killed my father and my mother! Now Straight Foretop is alone, but his hands are full of weapons. He will not go alive to the Soldier Coats!'

'Let the bastards have it, Lieutenant,' Wyuse screamed, lunging his horse at Conquering Bear.

'Fire!' bellowed Lieutenant Grattan.

Rifles crashed and Conquering Bear staggered. His brother Little Thunder fell mortally wounded.

Though badly . hurt, Conquering Bear attempted to pull Wyuse from his horse. Wyuse pulled a revolver and fired two bullets into his chest. Both howitzers fired. The shells tore through the lodges, and several were knocked down. Straight Foretop sent his war arrow thudding into the throat of Lieutenant Grattan, who, with a choking cry, tumbled from his mount.

Several hundred warriors raced howling out of the canebreaks to send clouds of arrows at the thirty soldiers, hitting most of them. They then swarmed over them with war clubs and lances.

Wyuse clapped spurs to his horse in a bid for freedom, only to find escape cut off by charging mounted warriors that had come up from the Oglala encampment. He leapt from his horse and sought escape inside Conquering Bear's lodge. Enraged warriors dragged him out and a war club descended on his head, scattering his brains over his face.

When the howitzers fired, Caspar, Tashunka and Little Singing Stream fought their frightened ponies for a few hundred feet before getting them under control. Then, white-faced, they looked at one another as the sounds of fighting fell to a few scattered shots, then to silence.

'It is done! Finished!' Tashunka's eyes flashed with satisfaction. Casper said, 'It is only begun, Tashunka. There will be big trouble over this killing. Pretty soon many Soldier Coats will be sent after the Lakotas.'

'There are not enough Soldier Coats at the

fort to fight us. It will take many weeks to bring enough from the other forts. By then we will be far away. Will our friend Cas be coming with us?'

Caspar shook his head. 'My father is a Soldier Coat Chief. Cas must go back to the fort. But Cas will tell the Big Soldier Coat Chief Fleming that it was Lieutenant Grattan and Wyuse who started the fight.'

'My heart is in the ground. But the door of my lodge will always be open to my friend Cas.'

For a long moment their glances held. This was a bitter parting for both boys. Then Caspar turned his pony alongside Little Singing Stream. He handed her the rawhide lead rope of the pack pony bearing his prized white buffalo robe. Little Singing Stream's brown eyes grew big with both awe and sadness.

She said quietly, 'This is a very big present, Cas ...' Caspar started to say something, swallowed hard, turned his pony and put it to a gallop. Tashunka, to hide his grief, shouted, 'Hoppo! Hoppo up!' and galloped toward the Oglala encampment. Little Singing Stream stared after Caspar. When her eyes brimmed with tears, she turned her pinto and raced off after Tashunka, leading the pack pony.

Private Turk was getting more fed up by the minute riding with a snotty, no-talking, brand new second lieutenant who had that faraway look in his eyes. Etiquette or no etiquette, he was bound he'd get the bastard talking. He said, 'Lieutenant! See that bend in the river down yonder?' Caspar nodded. 'Well, that's the north fork of the Platte River, an' a few miles further on, 'bout ten years ago, the Sioux massacred a Lieutenant Grattan and some soldiers.'

If he had expected to scare Caspar, he was due for a disappointment. 'I heard about that,' Caspar commented. 'The detail was composed of a Lieutenant Grattan, thirty troopers, and an Indian scout named Wyuse.'

'Yeah,' Turk admitted, a little miffed that his information was not new to Caspar. 'But Wyuse was a half-breed so he don't count none. Say, how come you knowed about that massacre, Lieutenant? They teach you about it at West Point?'

Caspar shook his head, his attention drawn toward the river. 'I saw that massacre, soldier. I was there.'

'You—you wuz there?' Turk spluttered.

'That's right! Here comes Jim Bridger with company.' He grinned broadly, his gray eyes sparkling with pleasure. 'Well, I'll be damned! He's got Sergeant Mike Hanna with him. Pull up, soldier.'

Private Turk sawed on the reins and set the brake. Caspar jumped down as Jim Bridger rode up with a broadly faced, grizzled sergeant who was leading a fine, saddled appaloosa gelding. Both men and horses were soaked from the recent rain.

'Welcome home, Lieutenant,' Sergeant Hanna grinned as he gave Caspar a stiff formal salute, which Caspar returned equally correctly. He then grasped Hanna's horny hand in both of his. 'It's great to see you again, Mike,' he exclaimed warmly. 'Like old times.'

'We're both a little wet, but the major sent me along with this here appaloosa, his welcome-home present, sir. He figured you'd be kinda tired riding a rock-hard supply wagon seat and'd be right glad to put your rump on a McClellan instead.'

Caspar gave the big horse a quick inspection, stroked its silken muzzle affectionately and asked, 'Has he got a name?'

'The major's already named him, subject to the Lieutenant's approval, of course,' Sergeant Hanna told him, secretly enjoying the small suspense he was handing Caspar.

'Oh, come on, Mike,' Caspar grinned. 'Let's have it. What name did Dad pick out?'

'Well, the major mulled over two or three names, but finally settled on one he thought the Lieutenant would like. He settled for Lakota.'

'Lakota,' Caspar's grin widened. He nodded approval. 'I like it! It fits him.' He swung into the saddle and added, 'I'd bet even money I know who put the idea in Dad's head to send you to meet me. A certain old timer named Mike Hanna.'

Hanna smoothed his dragoon mustache to hide a pleased grin. He said, 'In that you could be right, Lieutenant.'

Private Turk interrupted. 'Could I ask the Lieutenant a question?'

'Go right ahead, soldier,' Caspar returned, settling himself in the saddle.

Private Turk paused, having difficulty choosing the right words. 'Lieutenant, sir, you say you saw the Grattan massacre, and now I ain't doubtin' your word none at all, sir, but the Sioux killed all the other whites so how come they didn't kill you, too?'

Caspar threw a covert wink at Jim Bridger, who smothered a grin.

'That's a good question,' Caspar admitted. 'I think maybe the reason they spared me was because my mother's name was Pretty Valley. She was a full-blooded Oglala-Lakota Indian. Some people might even call me a half-breed. Thanks for the history lesson, soldier.'

He rode on with Sergeant Hanna.

Private Turk seemed about to swallow his Adam's apple. 'Now how in hell was I supposed to know his ma was a full-blooded Sioux?' he blurted out, indignantly.

Jim Bridger shifted his generous chaw of tobacco to his other cheek. He commented with his usual caustic humor, 'Sonny, out

13

here on the frontier it ain't bad advice fer a greenhorn ter keep his big yap shet! An' fer a piece o' free history, soljer, thar ain't no sech thing as a Sioux Injun. Most whites calls 'em Sioux, but they's really Lakotas. Of which the seven big tribes are the Oglalas, the Hunkpapas, the Minneconjous, the Sans Arcs, the Brules, the No Bows an' the Bad Faces. Sioux is a Lakota word meanin' cutthroat, which same a Lakota'd do to any enemy, after he'd first lifted his scalp, if he was real riled at him.'

CHAPTER TWO

The death scaffold stood in a small clearing among the pines. The red-blanketed body that had lain on the platform was gone. All that remained were the withered rawhide thongs that lashed the platform to the upright poles and the shrunken big intestine of a buffalo, stuffed with pemmican to sustain the deceased on the long journey to Wanagi Yata, the land of the Great Spirit.

A lonely grave with a red granite marker was at the base of the death scaffold. A green pine cone fell to the ground and a gray mountain squirrel with tufted ears jumped from a pine bough onto the death scaffold and thence to the ground to retrieve the cone.

14

Then it fled back up the death scaffold to the pine bough as Caspar and Sergeant Hanna rode up.

Sergeant Hanna said, 'The major thought you'd want to stop here, Lieutenant.'

'Thanks, Mike,' Caspar said. He tossed him his reins and dismounted, slowly looking over the empty death scaffold and the red granite marker. 'My father couldn't have picked a prettier spot.'

'You're right there, Lieutenant, and it's a sight better than that windswept cemetery at Fort Laramie. At first the major wrapped his lady in a red blanket and put her on the death scaffold as was the custom of her people. But he couldn't sleep none worrying about her, so he came back and buried her according to his own ways.'

Caspar removed his campaign hat, dropped to one knee in front of the red marker. His eyes read the epitaph chiseled in the red stone:

PRETTY VALLEY

Beloved wife of

Rufus Collins.
Capt. 3rd. U.S. Cavalry
1861

Caspar bowed his head and touched the

fingertips of his left hand to his forehead, the Lakota sign of deepest respect. Sunlight filtered through the pine branches overhead and emphasized the high cheekbones of his half Indian ancestry more vividly to Sergeant Hanna than he had been aware of before.

The recent storm had washed the accumulated June dust from the parapets and roofs of the buildings of Fort Laramie. Out on the broad parade ground, Corporal Big Mouth, a slit-eyed, unprepossessing Lakota, was ineffectually drilling a detail of Indian scouts, wearing blue tunics, breechcloths, Indian leggings and moccasins. Lone eagle feathers protruded through holes in the crowns of their black felt hats. They were armed with muzzleloading Enfield rifles which they shouldered in complete disarray. When the detail neared Regimental Headquarters, Corporal Big Mouth decided to show any white officers who might be watching that he was a fine corporal.

'Now you walk like real Soldier Coats!' he bellowed. 'Wan two free fo'; wan two free fo'.' The Indian scouts put a little cadence into their marching, but not much.

Captain William Fetterman, a lean, arrogant, ambitious career officer, came out of Headquarters with young Second Lieutenant George Ransome and paused to disdainfully watch Corporal Big Mouth and his sloppy Indian scouts. Captain Fetterman inhaled deeply on his thin, black cigar and shook his head. 'So long as orders are to enlist Indian scouts, they should have exempted Shoshones. They're not worth the powder to blow 'em to kingdom come. They'll run off howling at the first shot. Only one worth a damn is Corporal Big Mouth and he's a Sioux,' he remarked sardonically.

Second Lieutenant George Ransome, who on all occasions sought to emulate his idol, Captain Fetterman, snorted, 'It gripes the hell out of me to see any of those stinkin' red devils wearing United States Army uniforms, sir.'

'Better get used to it, mister, compliments of those great souls in the Bureau of Indian Affairs in Washington.'

'Like as not some night we'll all get our throats slit.'

'I've already mentioned that possibility to Major Collins. Needless to say, he didn't agree with me,' Captain Fetterman smiled thinly. His eyes narrowed as he saw Caspar and Sergeant Hanna ride in through the fort gates and added, 'Speaking of our beloved red brethren, Mr. Ransome, here comes the Academy's latest gift to Fort Laramie. As junior officer on the post, I'll leave you to do the honors.' He moved off swiftly toward officer's row.

Caspar and Sergeant Hanna rode up to Headquarters and dismounted. Caspar tossed

17

his reins to Sergeant Hanna and exchanged salutes with Lieutenant Ransome, who, with a slightly condescending smile, stepped forward and offered his hand. 'I'm George Ransome, lowly second lieutenant of A Troop. Welcome to Fort Desolation, Mr. Collins. My friends call me George.'

'Mine call me Caspar, among other things,' Caspar grinned, taking his hand. 'Is Major Collins inside?'

'Waiting with everything but the red carpet, Caspar.'

Caspar sensed an undertone of resentment beneath Lieutenant Ransome's friendly words.

'Knowing my Dad, he'll be leaning over backwards to show no partiality to this brand new second lieutenant. See you later, George.'

The friendliness left Lieutenant Ransome's eyes as he watched Caspar take the sentry's salute and disappear into Regimental Headquarters.

Major Rufus Collins was born in Council Bluffs, Iowa. He graduated from West Point Military Academy, class of 1838, and was posted to the Third Cavalry on the then western frontier, a dreary outpost duty with female companionship limited to dance hall girls whose advancing age had driven them westward. Seldom was a settler's daughter willing to move into a one-room shack and

18

live on the low pay of a second lieutenant. Second Lieutenant Rufus Collins had been a lonely young man until his horse threw him and left him lying in the forest with a broken leg near where some Oglala girls were picking wild plums. One of them found him. Her name was Pretty Valley. With the help of the other girls she cut sapplings, made a travois and transported the young lieutenant to the Oglala village where she nursed him back to health.

Major Rufus Collins felt a swift surge of pride as he watched Caspar ride up and dismount. He had sent the Academy a fine young man, but one who found his pleasures away from the fort, who preferred hunting, swimming and the companionship of Indians to his army playmates. Now, four years later, he was getting back a young man of obvious military bearing, and one who seemed to be able to hold his own even with a notorious Indian baiter like Lieutenant Ransome. But, the major knew, the Indian strain ran strongly in Caspar, and he wondered whether the Academy had been able to get him to fit this into the right perspective. The major was also a little apprehensive whether this strong Indian strain would allow him to accept Victoria. He smoothed his tunic over his broad shoulders and pulled it down smartly, passing his hand over his graying hair and sucking in his stomach. The major was forty-nine. When the orderly ushered in Caspar, the major was seated at his desk, every inch the commanding officer.

Caspar saluted smartly and announced, crisply, 'Second Lieutenant Caspar Collins reporting for duty, sir.' He handed over a long brown envelope. 'My orders, sir.'

Major Collins slit the long envelope with a hunting knife and glanced at the official document.

'Humph! Finished seventh in your class.'

'Yes, sir.'

The major glanced up, found Caspar staring at the wall above his head in the correct West Point posture. 'Better than I did, mister. Best I could manage was number seventeen.'

His eyes didn't return to the document. Instead they studied his son's face. His high cheekbones and his clear, slightly golden coloring reminded him strongly of Pretty Valley, but like his own, Caspar's eyes were gray, bordered by the thick black lashes of the Lakotas. He tossed the document on the desk, rose abruptly. 'At ease, mister. That takes care of the damned formalities. Come here and let me look at you.' He placed his hands on Caspar's shoulders, holding him at arm's length. 'Those four years at the Academy haven't hurt you, son. You're looking great.'

'You look pretty good yourself, Dad,'

Caspar rejoined with affection.

'A little older. A little grayer. Perhaps a little wiser.' He smiled, hesitating, seemingly embarrassed. 'Did you get my letter, Cas, the one telling you about Victoria Hunter?'

Caspar nodded and said quietly, 'It was delivered four days before graduation, Dad.' The major turned to his desk, seeking the right words, hoping he would find them. He put Caspar's orders in a drawer, then turned to face his son again.

'I meant no disrespect to your mother's memory, Caspar, but these past few years have been ...' He shook his head, his lips tightened, then took a deep breath and forged ahead. 'I met Victoria in St. Louis on my last furlough. She was a widow. Her late husband, Captain Arthur Hunter of the Second, was killed at Bull Run. I—I guess it was a case of two lonely people finding each other. Victoria is a fine lady, Caspar.'

Caspar put an affectionate arm about his father's shoulders.

'Bound to be if you picked her, Dad.'

All tension passed from the major's eyes, and he picked up his campaign hat and said, 'Come, I'll let you judge for yourself. By the way, you'll be assigned to Bachelor Officers' Quarters. Vic wanted you to live with us, but some of my officers might feel I was showing partiality to my son.'

'Which, of course, you would be, sir,'

Caspar grinned.

Victoria Collins was a willowy ash-blonde with wide green eyes. In her early twenties she must have been an outstanding beauty. Now, in her late thirties, she was still a very attractive woman. Victoria was an army brat, meaning that she was born and raised on army posts. Her world was populated with army types, so it was natural that at twenty-one she married one, First Lieutenant Arthur Hunter of the Second Cavalry.

Hers had not been a wildly romantic affair. Rather it had been a case of choosing a mate within a prescribed circle. She had known Arthur for seven years and had enjoyed his company more than that of any other eligible bachelor. She was very fond of him but she had never been deeply in love with him. That experience came when she met Major Rufus Collins on furlough from Fort Laramie, an area remote from the mud and blood of the current War between the States that so occupied the hearts and minds of most of the population both of the North and South.

Having no children from her marriage to Captain Arthur Hunter to bind her to her previous world, she had been fascinated by Major Rufus Collins' talk of forests and rivers, of great plains black with buffalo, of the Lakotas, Cheyennes and other Indian tribes. She had also sensed the great loneliness of the man and a similar loneliness, she realized, had always been locked deep within her own heart. Her aunt in St. Louis, with whom she had been staying, had been shocked clear out of her ample stays at her marrying a man who had once been married to an Indian woman. But she had no such misgivings. Rather, it seemed to add to the mystery, to the strange fascination, to the rugged individualism of this man.

Victoria was a happy woman, safe in the knowledge that she was greatly loved by the major. The only small cloud on her horizon was the major's son, Caspar. How would a half-Indian accept her in place of his own mother?

Regan, the major's combination orderly and cook, knocked on the bedroom door to inform her that the major and lieutenant were coming down Officers' Row.

'Is the lemonade ready, Regan?' she asked, trying to keep the excitement from her voice.

'Three pitchers of it, ma'am.'

'Good,' she called. 'Please service it quickly. Lieutenant Collins is bound to be thirsty after his long ride.'

Presently she heard the front door open and the boots of two big men scrape the bare boards, becoming muffled as they trod on the bear and deer skins scattered about the big room.

'Vic! Vic! Caspar's here,' she heard the major call.

'I'll be right out, Rufus,' she called back
She made a hasty check of her appearance in
the long mirror, took a deep breath and
entered the living room.

The major said proudly, 'Vic, this is
Caspar. Caspar, your stepmother.'

Victoria paused, gave Caspar a warm
almost shy smile, as she embraced him and
kissed him on the cheek.

'Caspar,' she said softly, 'I've always felt
the name Mother to be very special and
belonging to only one person. Won't you
please call me Vic?'

Any preconceived reservations about his
father's new wife melted immediately. He
said, quietly, 'I would like that, Vic. Dad
you didn't tell me you married a real beauty.'

'Caspar,' Vic flushed. 'I'm thirty-eight
years old, but I am still female enough to
enjoy polite flattery.'

'It wasn't polite flattery, Vic, was it, Dad?'

'Why, no, not at all, Vic. I think Caspar
joins me in considering you a very lovely
woman.'

Regan entered from the kitchen with a tray
of glasses and two pitchers of lemonade,
which he placed on the table near Victoria.

'Caspar, you remember Regan?'

Caspar held out his hand. 'Used to be
Corporal Regan, guidon bearer of B Troop,
right?'

'Right, sir. I retired last year, but somehow

24

couldn't get used to living away from an army post. Good to have you back, Lieutenant.'

As he retired to the kitchen, Vic said, 'Well, goodness me, let's not stand on ceremony. Do sit down and have some lemonade. Your father was quite surprised to get your letter saying that you'd take your graduation furlough here at Fort Laramie,' she said, handing Caspar a tall glass of lemonade.

'In my day, graduation furloughs were either spent on a bender in New York or on a honeymoon,' Major Collins chuckled.

'Don't tell me there wasn't some special girl, Caspar,' Victoria teased.

'Well, there was one I liked pretty well, but not enough to give up posting to the Indian frontier. I wanted to see you again, Dad, to show Vic what sort of wild Indian she'd inherited, and I wanted to spend my furlough looking up old friends.'

'Not many old friends left, I'm afraid, Caspar. More than half of the regiment was transferred back East to the Army of the Potomac. Just a few you'd remember, like Sergeant Mike Hanna, Regan and Cochoran, who still runs the sutler's store.'

'I meant the Oglalas, Dad,' Caspar replied quietly. 'The real friends I grew up with like Tashunka, He Dog, Lone Bear and Little Singing Stream, who must be a grown woman by now.'

The major frowned and emptied his glass. A shadow passed through Victoria's eyes as she glanced at her husband. This was a possibility they had discussed, a possibility they'd been afraid of. He placed his empty glass on the table and began filling a blackened briar pipe. He said, 'We've a sort of truce with the Lakotas and the Cheyennes and, as all the frontier forts are woefully undermanned, I hope it lasts. Roughly, they'll give us no trouble so long as we prevent the white buffalo hunters from crossing the Powder River and keep all whites out of Pa Sapa, their sacred Black Hills.' He paused to light his pipe. 'At present, the Oglala lodges are on the Tongue River near the crossing of the Boseman Trail. Tashunka made his first kill in a fight with the Shoshones and is now a warrior. His father, who was a holy man, has taken the name of Worm and has given his warrior name to his son. Tashunka is now known as Crazy Horse.'

'Crazy Horse,' Caspar smiled and nodded. 'It is an honorable name. His father was a great warrior in his day. It will be good to see Tashunka—I mean Crazy Horse—again. Been almost ten years since that fool Grattan fired his guns through the Brule lodges on the Shell River.'

The major coughed, and reddened. 'Caspar, Lieutenant Grattan was Vic's brother.' Caspar shot Victoria an agonized look. 'Sorry, Vic. I—I didn't know.'

'It's all right, Caspar. I don't suppose your father mentioned that my maiden name was Grattan?' she smiled graciously.

'Matter of fact, Dad didn't. But it wasn't really your brother's fault, Vic. He was new on the frontier. He had a drunken scout with him named Wyuse. Wyuse started the massacre. He yelled to your brother to open fire, then tried to ride down Chief Conquering Bear! This useless tragedy and others like the Battle of the Blue Water in '55 and Sumner's Expedition against the Cheyennes in '57 were added reasons why I asked to be posted out here.' He grinned, shook his head. 'Didn't mean to get up on a soapbox, Dad, it's just that I thought the Lakotas, or Sioux as the Army calls them, and their Cheyenne cousins'd listen to an officer who was half Oglala and whose heart felt good toward their people.'

'"Whose heart felt good toward their people."' Vic exclaimed, enchanted. 'Why, Caspar, what a beautiful way of expressing it.'

'There's a lot of beauty and honesty in the Lakota language, Vic. No subterfuges. For instance, when a Lakota disagrees violently with something, he will say, "I set my face against this bad thing." Then he'll walk away.'

Major Collins nodded agreement. He said,

'I wish we were as forthright among ourselves. Probably save a lot of misunderstandings.'

'Might even have averted this horrible war with the Confederacy, Rufus,' Vic commented.

'Possibly, Vic. But both sides were pretty proud. Too proud! By the way, Caspar, George Ransome is taking a patrol out tomorrow. You can ride with him as far as the Powder River.'

'I met him outside Headquarters, just now, Dad. Seemed like a nice fellow.'

'Mr. Ransome will season out in time, I hope,' the major replied, noncommitally. 'But, at the moment, he holds to an opinion all too prevalent among some of our officers, that the only good Indian is—'

'A dead one?' Caspar finished. His father nodded, touched a sulfur match to his pipe, which had gone out.

'Mind if I enlighten the gentleman?' Caspar grinned.

'Nooo, not if you're tactful about it, Caspar. Remember, Mr. Ransome outranks you. I think I'll take the added precaution of detailing Sergeant Hanna along to help keep the peace.' He blew a perfect smoke ring. 'Tell Chief Spotted Tail my patrols will continue to keep the white buffalo hunters east of the Powder and out of the Lakota's sacred Black Hills.'

CHAPTER THREE

Three death scaffolds stood out gauntly in a ravine among the lower slopes of the Black Hills. The red blankets that covered the quiet occupants were weather whipped into shreds. The wind came sighing down the granite cliffs, through the stately pines, causing the scaffold poles to creak. A fluttering of red blanket shreds and occasional small dust puffs were kicked up along the narrow trail below.

The patrol moved along the trail at a canter, raising its own cloud of dust. Jim Bridger rode a hundred yards in advance. Caspar rode beside Lieutenant Ransome, followed by Sergeant Hanna. After him rode the platoon, thirty bronzed troopers in double file with Corporal Muldoon riding left front carrying the guidon of A Troop. The rear was brought up by two civilian packers and four pack mules.

Lieutenant Ransome cast a disdainful glance at the three gaunt death scaffolds upslope among the pines.

'Those death scaffolds give me the crawling snakes!' he remarked harshly. 'Hell of a way to get rid of the dead.'

'The Lakotas and Cheyennes believe if you bury a man in the ground his spirit will remain forever earthbound and he'll never be able to make the long journey to Wanagi Yata, their Spirit Land. It ties in with their religion, George,' Caspar explained quietly.

'I've heard all that foofaraw, Caspar. But put a man's body in the hot sun for three days and it'll stink up the whole area. What the Black Hills needs is a first rate forest fire!'

Caspar's eyes narrowed slightly. 'Then you must be a devotee of the suttee, George.'

'Suttee? What the devil's that?'

'In India, when a Hindu dies, he's cremated. The richer the Hindu, the bigger his funeral pyre.'

'Now that makes sense—completely sanitary.'

'There is only one small drawback to it, George.'

'Eh, what's that?'

'At the height of the blaze, his widow has to fling herself into the flames. Little rough on the widow, wouldn't you say?'

Lieutenant Ransome gave a short laugh. 'In my next life, providing there is such a thing, remind me not to come back as a Hindu woman, Caspar.'

'Be glad to, George, providing you don't forget to remind me to remind you.'

Behind them, Sergeant Hanna was riding close enough to overhear the conversation. Before leaving, Major Collins had cautioned him to try to keep the peace between Lieutenant Collins and Lieutenant Ransome.

30

An unnecessary warning, Sergeant Hanna decided, since young Lieutenant Collins hadn't allowed Lieutenant Ransome's barbed mockery to get under his skin.

When the patrol passed north of Pumpkin Butte, the mountain trail gave way to far reaching grassy slopes that lost themselves in the distant haze hanging over the Belle Fourche River.

At an arm signal from Lieutenant Ransome, the patrol slowed to a walk.

'It's only about eleven miles to the Belle Fourche River where we'll make camp,' Lieutenant Ransome said, removing his campaign hat and wiping his forehead on his sleeve. 'Territory look familiar to you, Caspar?'

Caspar let his eyes rove over the vast sea of grass before replying. 'The physical characteristics haven't changed, George, just the population.'

'What, no Indians?' Lieutenant Ransome prodded.

Caspar shook his head. 'No sign of buffalo, George. Only five years ago there were big herds here, sometimes as many as twenty or thirty thousand. Hills covered with shaggy brown.'

'There was a big buffalo herd just south of Pumpkin Butte last fall, Cas. I went along with a group of regular hide hunters. We knocked over nearly four thousand of the brutes.' Caspar's mouth tightened, but when he spoke his voice betrayed none of his pent-up anger. 'So they collected about four thousand hides. What happened to the meat?'

'Oh, we stuffed on juicy buffalo hump steaks, all we could eat.' He shrugged. 'The rest we left. Something bothering you, Caspar?'

'The Indians only kill what they need. The girls and squaws follow the hunters, they skin the buffalo and cut up this meat, pile it on travois and drag it to camp to be made into smoked jerky and pemmican. Nothing is wasted. The buffalo means food, warmth and shelter to the Indians. Kill off the herds and they face starvation.'

'Which'll force them to come into the reservations where we can keep an eye on them.'

'You're wrong, George. If the hide hunters keep up this wild slaughter, they'll set the Lakotas and the Cheyennes on the warpath!'

'Let 'em!' Lieutenant Ransome jeered. 'Captain Fetterman said give him fifty troopers and he'd ride through the whole Sioux nation!'

'Did the captain mention anything about riding back?' Caspar asked sharply.

Lieutenant Ransome guffawed, 'I'll tell him you asked. I'm sure he'll appreciate the question.' He glanced sideways and was amused to note he had finally gotten under

Caspar's skin.

Sergeant Hanna, who had heard the altercation with rising apprehension, urged his mount forward.

'Lieutenant,' he said, 'Why don't I take the packers on ahead to Belle Fourche? We can have camp set up and smudge fires going. If the wind drops, those blasted mosquitoes'll move in in regimental formation.'

'Good idea, Sergeant,' Lieutenant Ransome replied, 'carry on.' Sergeant Hanna saluted, turned to Caspar. 'A few years back, Lieutenant, you'd spend half your time swimming in the North Platte. How about coming along for a quick dip in the Belle Fourche afore the mosquitoes move in?'

'Right with you, Sergeant,' Caspar grinned. 'See you later, George.' Sergeant Hanna bellowed for the packers to move up with their pack mules.

As they moved out at a canter ahead of the patrol Caspar said, 'If I ever have a daughter, Mike, I'll hire you. Mrs. Sergeant Mike Hanna, chaperon!'

'Might take you up on that job, Lieutenant, I might at that,' he grinned.

The sun hung low in the western sky, turning the broad, shallow waters of the Belle Fourche to gleaming, reddish gold as Caspar and Sergeant Hanna came out of the water and donned their uniforms. Several troopers rode down the bank, leading the patrol's horses to water in the river. Jim Bridger rode his horse into the water near where Caspar and Sergeant Hanna were pulling on their boots. He sat slumped in the saddle while his horse drank.

Caspar called, 'Hey, Jim, why don't you take a swim? The water's great.'

'You ain't catchin' me in no river, Lieutenant,' he chortled.

'I got down wind from you today, Jim,' Sergeant Hanna chuckled, stamping into his boots. 'You could sure use a bath.'

Jim shifted his tobacco chaw to the other cheek and grinned, 'Took me a bath last spring, Mike, at Sand Creek. 'Tain't healthful to over do a good thing. Besides, I gotta piroot 'round a bit to make sure that ain't no Shosone war parties huntin' for you fellers' hair.'

The sun dipped below the western horizon and the long summer twilight took over. The wind dropped and clouds of mosquitoes moved in. Small knots of troopers squatted around low smudge fires, swatting at mosquitoes as they ate their jerky stew. Horses and mules on picket lines stamped their hoofs, swished their tails, and tossed their heads to rid themselves of the pests. The trooper on sentry had the added duty of feeding four smudge fires to ease their torment.

Caspar, Lieutenant Ransome, and Sergeant

Hanna squatted at one smudge fire, eating supper. Their attention was caught as Jim Bridger rode in, put his horse on picket, and unsaddled. At times Jim Bridger was a singing man, songs mostly confined to ribald ditties. As he worked and swatted mosquitoes, he sang:

'Oh, I'm a ringtailed renegado
An' the dangest fightin' fool.
I've licked muh share o' grizzly bars
An' ain't never been tuh school.

Born high up the Shinin' Mountains
An' raised on panther's milk,
Stole a squaw from the Kiowas
An' her skin was slick as silk.

Now, her name wuz Burnin' Blanket
An' her maw's wuz Burnin' Brook.
Her paw was Burnin' Britches
EEE-yow, how thet gal could cook.'

'No wonder the Indians call him Big Throat,' Lieutenant Ransome commented with a cold grin. 'Always wondered why, when it comes to picking scouts, the Army always selects the dirtiest old reprobates they can find.'

Caspar hid his rising resentment under a friendly grin. He said, 'They don't pick scouts for parade smartness, George. Jim is

35

about the best there is and hasn't ever been known to run from a fight. The Indians like him, too. When I was a kid I spent many a night in the great lodge circles of the Lakotas and Cheyennes while Jim let go with his ballads. They didn't understand what they were about, but they'd keep him singing till he was hoarse.'

'You should hear him when he's got a quart of rotgut under his belt. That's an education in itself, Lieutenant. Heard tell the saloons in Denver'll give him free whiskey just so long as he sings,' Sergeant Hanna chuckled.

Meanwhile, Jim had filled his tin plate with jerky stew at the cookfire and his tin mug with coffee. He came over to the smudge fire and squatted opposite Lieutenant Ransome.

'Made a wide circle o' the camp, both sides o' the river, Lieutenant,' he said to Lieutenant Ransome. 'Didn't see nothin' but a little dust kicked up to the south-east. Tweren't big enough for a raidin' Crow or Shoshone war party. Figger like as not it's some Injuns huntin' elk which are running purty good right now, thet or maybe a small party o' white buffalo hide hunters. So you ain't got nothin' to worry 'bout 'cept these pesky mosquitoes.' He slapped at his neck. Lieutenant Ransome nodded acceptance of Jim's report with a mocking light in his eyes.

'Are we to gather from your somewhat ribald aria, that you are partial to squaws,

36

Mr. Bridger?' he asked silkily.

'In that you'd be kerrect, Lieutenant,' Jim replied evenly. 'Got me a squaw with Black Kettle's Northern Cheyennes. Name o' Yaller Moon. She kin run like a deer an' swim like a fish. Purty as a picture, too.'

Lieutenant Ransome raised an amused eyebrow. 'Any other social graces?'

Caspar's anger erupted. He ignored a warning look from Sergeant Hanna and answered for Jim Bridger. 'Just the ones that count. Like being completely loyal to her man, be he white or red, taking care of his every want, and dying for him if need be. What more would you demand of a woman, Mr. Ransome?'

That he was not among friends worried the lieutenant not at all. However, he did realize he had overstepped the mark, remembering that Caspar's father was his commanding officer. He placed a friendly hand on Caspar's shoulder. 'Hey, take it easy, Caspar,' he grinned. 'As an officer on the frontier I want to learn all I can about our Indian friends. I was merely asking Mr. Bridger his views on squaws.'

'Now, you've heard Jim's and you've heard mine,' Caspar returned.

'True,' Lieutenant Ransom nodded, lighting a cigar. 'But I haven't heard from Sergeant Hanna. How about it, Sergeant, are you partial to squaws, too?'

Sergeant Hanna frowned, stroked his dragoon moustache. 'Lieutenant,' he said, 'When I retire from this man's army an' draw my forty dollars a month pension, I'm going to build me a log cabin an' share it with the prettiest Injun gal I can find. Respectfully, sir.'

'If you can't fight 'em, marry 'em. Well, that's one way of solving the Indian problem,' Lieutenant Ransome commented drily.

A shouted warning from the sentry at the picket line alerted the corporal of the guard that four Indians were approaching.

'Only four Injuns. No call fer appearin' warlike, Lieutenant.' The corporal of the guard and four troopers snatched up their carbines and started upslope toward the picket lines. Lieutenant Ransome shouted for them to stay back, but to be on the alert.

Jim Bridger started up the slope, followed by Caspar, Lieutenant Ransome, and Sergeant Hanna.

CHAPTER FOUR

Four young Indians rode over the ridge and down the slope, heading for the river. They led four pack ponies. Each had the carcass of an elk lashed across its back. All were armed with muzzleloading Enfield rifles, their bare chests adorned with bearclaw necklaces. They were dressed in breechcloths, deerskin leggins and moccasins. Their hair was worn in two braids bound up with beaver fur. Three wore eagle feathers in their hair, marking them as warriors. The leader, lighter skinned than his companions, whose hair was almost a light-brown, wore the feathers of a red-backed hawk in his hair.

In an aside to Caspar, Jim Bridger said, 'Lieutenant, that fine looking Injun on the buckskin's yer old friend, Crazy Horse.' He raised his left hand, palm outward, in the peace sign of the Oglala's. Crazy Horse returned the gesture and drew rein.

'Big Throat is a long ways from the lodges of Black Kettle's Cheyennes,' Crazy Horse remarked.

'Be going back there in three moons,' Jim Bridger replied.

'That is good.' Crazy Horse's face showed his pleasure. 'The heart of Yellow Moon is troubled because her lodge is empty.' He was about to say more, but suddenly his eyes fastened on Caspar, narrowing quizzically.

Caspar stepped forward, and smiled. 'Have so many snows gone by that Tashunka has forgotten his friend Cas?'

In one movement Crazy Horse thrust his rifle into his war rope and dismounted from his buckskin. Next, he engaged in the Lakota crossed-hands handshake. 'Hohahe, Cas, you have come back to your people,' he exclaimed, delighted.

'For a little while,' Caspar returned, with marked affection. Lieutenant Ransome watched the meeting with cold amusement.

'He Dog, Lone Bear, Little Big Man,' Crazy Horse shouted, 'Cas is here!' He Dog and Lone Bear leapt from their mounts and went through the crossed hands greeting with Caspar, grinning broadly. However, Little Big Man made no move to welcome Caspar. He remained sitting on his horse, his narrow eyes dark and unfriendly. His voice lashed out harshly, 'Cas now is a Soldier Coat, why is this?'

There was both anger and authority in the retort of Crazy Horse. 'Little Big Man, hear me! The father of Cas is a Soldier Coat Chief! Now our friend Cas is also a Soldier Coat Chief! To follow in the moccasin tracks of his father is the honorable thing to do!' He turned apologetically to Caspar, smiling. 'Cas must close his ears to the bad mouth of Little Big Man. His mother was frightened by a wolverine. Cas will ride with his friends Lone Bear, He Dog and Crazy Horse to the Oglala village?'

'Cas will ride with his friends. But first they must eat. There is jerky stew and hot coffee ready,' Caspar said.

Crazy Horse shook his head. 'We are in a big hurry to return to the Oglala village, for

40

tomorrow when the sun is in the middle. Little Singing Stream will take the woman's name of Evening Star.'

'Evening Star,' Caspar echoed in pleased surprise. 'Did Chief Spotted Tail choose this name?'

Crazy Horse shook his head. He Dog, who was a friendly, laughing young man who loved a joke chuckled, *'Hou! Hou!* Her father chose the name of Deerfoot Woman, but Little Singing Stream made such a big noise against it Chief Spotted Tail closed his ears and let her choose Evening Star.'

Crazy Horse placed a hand on Caspar's shoulder, saying softly, 'The white buffalo robe Cas gave her was her biggest present, Cas.'

'I'll saddle up for you, Lieutenant,' Sergeant Hanna grinned broadly and hurried toward the picket line.

Whooping and plying their wrist whips Caspar and his Oglala companions forded the Belle Fourche, gained the far bank, and quickly vanished in the blue evening haze.

Lieutenant Ransome stood on the eastern bank of the river and disdainfully watched after them. With him were Jim Bridger and Sergeant Hanna. Jim Bridger glanced at Lieutenant Ransome and didn't like what he saw. He decided that a little knifing of his least favorite officer was in order.

'See what I mean, Lieutenant,' he drawled.

41

'Treat them Injuns like they wuz equals an' you couldn't want fer finer friends.'

'Equals, ha!' Lieutenant Ransome jeered. 'All I saw was four treacherous, stinking Sioux!'

Jim Bridger spat disgustedly and walked away. Sergeant Hanna followed.

'Sergeant Hanna!' Lieutenant Ransome snapped.

'Lieutenant?'

Lieutenant Ransome's eyes were still looking across the river where Caspar and his Oglala friends had vanished. He said, 'Tell me, Sergeant, do you agree with Jim Bridger or with your commanding officer?'

'With neither of you, respectfully, sir.'

Lieutenant Ransome turned sharply, glared coldly at Sergeant Hanna. 'Explain that, Sergeant.'

'Well, sir, that Little Big Man is treacherous as a rattlesnake. Were I a red man or white I wouldn't trust him further'n I could throw a buffalo. But there's nothing treacherous about Crazy Horse, Lone Bear, or He Dog—otherwise they wouldn't have been boyhood friends of Lieutenant Collins.'

'That was ten years ago. Since then Crazy Horse, He Dog and Lone Bear have become warriors, meaning they've made their kills. If Mr. Collins continues that old friendship, he must have a wish.'

'A wish, Lieutenant?' Sergeant Hanna

asked warily.

'A death wish. That will be all, Sergeant.'

After hours of hard riding, Caspar and his Oglala friends put their foam flecked horses over a rise, and there below was the Oglala village, two hundred lodges arranged in seven lodge circles, strung along the west bank of the Tongue River. Crazy Horse glanced at the sun. It was almost overhead. He shouted to Caspar, '*Wi* is almost in the middle, Cas. We must hurry!'

Plying their wrist whips, the party raced down the slope, past the six hundred ponies of the great pony herd, being watched over by young boys. When they crossed the Tongue they were met by squaws and boys who took their horses and pack animals. Crazy Horse moved off on the run through the camp with Caspar at his heels, followed by He Dog, Lone Bear and Little Big Man.

The perimeter of the great lodge circle of Chief Spotted Tail was crowded with warriors, squaws, and young girls. The latter were bare-breasted but in their best beaded doeskin breechcloths to witness the giving of Little Singing Stream her woman's name.

Because Crazy Horse was an important warrior, the crowd opened to permit him, Caspar, He Dog, Lone Bear and Little Big Man to move to the front. The girls cast shy, inviting smiles at Crazy Horse but they lost them when they saw Caspar in his uniform.

Dark looks were tossed at him by the nearby warriors. More were cast his way as Little Big Man moved among the crowd, whispering and pointing at Caspar.

Crazy Horse turned to the immediate crowd. His voice was strong, commanding. 'Hear me! Close your ears against the bad words of Little Big Man.'

'Cas wears a Soldier Coat!' Little Big Man jeered. 'His father is a Soldier Chief!'

Crazy Horse put a hand on Caspar's shoulder. 'Cas is my friend! His mother was Pretty Valley, the daughter of Iron Hand. His heart feels good toward the Oglalas. They are his own people!'

Hostile looks vanished from the immediate warriors. Sly glances came from several young girls. Caspar returned the looks with friendly nods. Then he felt the hand of Crazy Horse on his shoulder. He said softly, 'The eyes of Cas should now be on the lodge of Chief Spotted Tail, for soon Little Singing Stream will appear.'

CHAPTER FIVE

Caspar looked across the wide lodge circle at the lodge of Chief Spotted Tail. This lodge was larger than the others. The door flap of the lodge was closed. Spotted Tail's war pony was tethered outside, and on a wooden frame were hung his war lance, his bow and quiver of arrows, his rifle and buffalo hide shield.

Seated cross-legged before the lodge was Worm, the holy man and father of Crazy Horse. He wore a buffalo horn headress, and shook his bone rattles while he sang a brave song about a Lakota woman who fought and killed two raiding Crow warriors. The chanting of Worm was taken up by the spectators who crowded the perimeter of the great lodge circle.

Presently, the door flap of the lodge was thrown open and Chief Spotted Tail stepped out, a tall, lean warrior in his early forties. He wore the full eagle-feathered war-bonnet. Over his left arm was draped the hide of the white buffalo calf that Caspar had shot ten years ago. The inside had been scraped smooth and was covered with sacred paintings. In his right hand he carried the long, feathered, ceremonial lance.

When Little Singing Stream appeared, the chanting rose in volume. Caspar caught his breath in open admiration as he stared at the girl whom he hadn't seen since the Grattan Massacre on the Shell River ten years ago. Now she was tall and slender, her skin a light golden hue. Her glossy black hair hung down in two braids bound up with beaded beaver fur. The center part of her hair was painted vermilion in the old Lakota way. She wore a tan, doeskin breechcloth, fringed and worked with small porcupine quills, beads, and small moccasins to match. A necklace of red, blue and yellow beads hung between her full firm young breasts.

Crazy Horse shot a side glance at Caspar, saw his fixed stare across the great lodge circle at Little Singing Stream, smiled and said, 'Many strong warriors will seek her for a wife.'

Caspar, his eyes still on Little Singing Stream, said, 'Any man would want her for a wife. There is no maiden more beautiful.'

Crazy Horse's look sharpened, saw that Caspar's words were sincere and was pleased to discover that during the ten year gap in their friendship, Caspar had not become contaminated with the common white man's prejudice toward all Indians.

Chief Spotted Tail raised his feathered ceremonial lance horizontally above his head and Worm, the holy man, put down his bone rattles, and the chanting sank to a whisper and died. The voice of Spotted Tail was clear and strong.

'Hear my words!' he said. 'This holy day my daughter, Little Singing Stream, has become a woman and shall now be given the woman's name of Evening Star.'

He handed his ceremonial lance to Worm, then draped the white buffalo calf robe over the shoulders of his daughter. The robe reached almost to her small, moccasined feet while the head formed a white hood over her glossy black hair. Worm handed the ceremonial lance back to Chief Spotted Tail, who pointed it sharply skyward.

Throbbing drumming broke the silence with a measured cadence. The warriors in the perimeter of the great lodge circle set up a chanting of *hoyes-hoyes* while the squaws and young girls joined in with a shrill keening.

With feathered ceremonial lance held high, Chief Spotted Tail began a stately march around the inner side of the great lodge perimeter, followed by Evening Star, her wide, soft brown eyes smiling proudly, for this was the biggest day of her life. The smile left her eyes when she passed Caspar, for she saw only the hated uniform and failed to recognize the man wearing it. Her smile flashed back on when she passed Crazy Horse.

Four times Chief Spotted Tail and Evening Star made the circle in the old Lakota ceremonial way. Then they reentered the great lodge and closed the flap door.

Caspar touched the arm of Crazy Horse and said, 'How soon may Cas talk with Evening Star?'

For a moment Crazy Horse frowned, as if scenting a rival. Then he placed a friendly hand on Caspar's shoulder and said, 'Crazy Horse will take his friend Cas to a place where

47

they can watch for Evening Star when she returns from swimming in the river.'

A bend in the Tongue River beyond some riffles formed a deep pool, edged by mossy banks that were overhung by willows and cottonwoods. Evening Star, who had been swimming under water, broke the surface, brushed back her wealth of blue black hair and squeezed the water from her eyes. She was quickly surrounded by a swarm of laughing, squealing girls who began splashing water at her. Evening Star returned the splashing. Then, outgunned, she dove like an otter and headed for the mossy bank, pursued by her playmates.

Upon gaining the mossy bank, Evening Star was quickly surrounded by her laughing companions who vied with one another for the honor of squeezing the water from her thick hair, of combing it with buffalo bone combs and fashioning it into two long braids.

A nubile fifteen-year-old named Brown Otter said slyly, 'The ears of Brown Otter hear that of all the strong warriors, Evening Star has eyes only for Crazy Horse.'

'Crazy Horse is a strong warrior. Someday he will be a big man among the Oglalas,' Evening Star replied evasively.

Deep Waters, an older girl with a practical turn of mind said, 'It is well known that Crazy Horse is not rich like many others who will want Evening Star for a wife. Will he have enough horses, blankets and bullets to buy her from Chief Spotted Tail? Besides that, Chief Spotted Tail will not look with favor on Crazy Horse because he brought a Soldier Coat to the Great Lodge Circle.'

Evening Star looked worried. 'That was a foolish thing for Crazy Horse to do.'

'It was not!' young Brown Otter piped up. 'Because Crazy Horse told us that the mother of the Soldier Coat was an Oglala, that her name was Pretty Valley.'

'It was Cas?' Evening Star cried in quick excitement.

'Yes,' Brown Otter cried. 'The name of the Soldier Coat was Cas!'

Upstream, Caspar and Crazy Horse lounged on the moss in a small glade beneath the willows by the river trail. Caspar lay on his stomach, puffing on his pipe. Crazy Horse sat cross-legged, his back against a cottonwood, pulled a small deerskin sack from his breech-cloth that was filled with *kniknik*, a powdered red bark from the willow, and started to fill his stone pipe. Caspar offered his own tobacco pouch. 'That *kniknik* would kill a grizzly bear. Try some good tobacco for a change,' he grinned. Crazy Horse shook his head and continued to fill his pipe.

'There are only three good things the white man makes in the eyes of the Lakotas: guns, bullets and blankets,' he said bitterly.

'What about coffee, sugar, molasses, fancy beads—these are also made by the white man,' Caspar reminded him. 'Crazy Horse, the world is changing. Ways must be found for the Indian and the white man to stop hating each other, to live together in peace. Cas knows this is the Land of the Lakotas and that—' He stopped as Crazy Horse raised a hand for silence.

'The ears of Cas have lost their sharpness from living too long with the Soldier Coats or they would have heard the girls returning from swimming.' There was veiled amusement in his voice. Caspar lifted his head and heard the distant laughter of the girls along the river trail. He tapped out his pipe, rose, ground the hot embers under his boot heel, his eyes fixed on the willow-screened trail.

Presently three girls, their long hair dripping wet, appeared along the river trail. They were followed by Evening Star, Brown Otter and Deep Waters. All wore only breechcloths and moccasins.

'*Hohahe!* Evening Star,' Crazy Horse called, rising. 'There is someone here for your eyes to see.'

The girls stopped, then Evening Star moved toward Caspar. Brown Otter and Deep Waters continued on their way, giggling, with occasional backward glances.

Evening Star walked to Caspar, her wet

braided hair glistening beside her proud full breasts. Her eyes were soft and tender.

Caspar said, 'Have so many snows gone by that Little Singing Stream had forgotten her friend Cas?'

She placed a hand on each of his shoulders and said, 'The heart of Evening Star is sad because four times she walked the great lodge circle and each time her eyes saw only the hated Soldier Coat and not her friend Cas.'

She rubbed her nose affectionately against Cas's nose in the Lakota way. It was all Caspar could do to keep from folding her in his arms. He said, 'The pictures of Tashunka and Little Singing Stream were always in my head.'

Evening Star smiled and asked, 'And what picture do the eyes of Cas see now?'

'They see a woman whose beauty glows like the moon in the darkness. A woman whose moccasin tracks Cas will always follow.'

Evening Star caught her breath, her smile became warmer at Caspar's indirect proposal of marriage.

Crazy Horse remarked amiably, 'Many will follow her moccasin tracks, Cas, including Crazy Horse.'

'Our buffalo scouts have returned,' Evening Star informed them with laughter in her eyes. 'They reported a big herd near Rosebud River. Tomorrow at first sun the Oglalas will begin the buffalo hunt, and the moccasins of Evening Star will leave big tracks.' She turned and ran after her companions.

Caspar turned to Crazy Horse. 'Will this wanting of Evening Star for a wife be a bad thing between Cas and Crazy Horse?'

Crazy Horse said quietly, 'The only bad thing that can come between Cas and Crazy Horse would be if Cas lead his Soldier Coats against the Lakotas.'

Caspar gave Crazy Horse a level look. 'That bad thing will never happen if Crazy Horse listens to the words of Cas, and Cas listens to the words of his friend Crazy Horse.'

Crazy Horse considered Caspar's words for a moment, then, with faint amusement in his eyes, he held out his hand and said, 'Crazy Horse will try some of the white man's smoking tobacco.' Caspar grinned and handed over his tobacco pouch.

Sunup found the Oglalas on the trail to the Rosebud. Ahead and on both sides rode the *akacitas*, Oglala police who kept the young hotheads from whipping their ponies and whooping, as they might stampede the buffalo and ruin the hunt. Next rode the hunters, and after them came the girls and squaws on their ponies. Long poles were lashed to the sides of the ponies, which later would form travois to transport the buffalo hides and meat to the camp where the meat would be dried and smoked. Behind them rode more warriors to protect them from roving bands of Crows or Shoshones, who would make a sudden slashing attack and steal young girls and be gone before the main force was aware of the raid.

Caspar rode knee-to-knee with Lone Bear and He Dog. Little Big Man rode just ahead. He glanced back at the Sharp's muzzleloader carbine in Caspar's saddleboot and jeered, 'That Sharp's muzzleloader of Cas will kill maybe one buffalo, and while he is reloading the herd will have stampeded far away. Cas should be riding with the women.'

Crazy Horse rode up and wedged in between Caspar and He Dog. He carried two bows and two quivers filled with hunting arrows.

'Cas will not need his muzzleloading carbine,' he said in reproof to Little Big Man. 'He used to out shoot me with the bow and arrow.' He handed the bow and quiver of arrows to Caspar. Caspar slung the quiver of arrows over his shoulder and tested the tension of the bowstring.

'Cas has not forgotten how to use these things,' he grinned. Crazy Horse said maliciously, 'If Little Big Man were a buffalo, he would soon have three of Cas' arrows in his back!'

Little Big Man glared at them both, then urged his horse on ahead. Crazy Horse said drily, 'Cas must watch Little Big Man, there is no good in him. Crazy Horse will watch him also.'

'So will He Dog,' He Dog growled.

'Also Lone Bear,' Lone Bear echoed.

'With such friends, Cas has no worries in his head,' Caspar rejoined. 'Little Big Man always made much noise but did very little.'

The cavalcade kicked up dust clouds, and the smells of horses, rawhide, and humanity were strong in the air. These things had a strange effect upon Caspar, momentarily making him forget that he was an officer in the United States Army and dropping him back ten years ago to when he rode with Tashunka, He Dog and Little Singing Stream. He could feel the wild freedom surging through his blood. The old excitement of the chase was back. Also, there was Evening Star who had grown into a woman whose calm beauty had swept him off his feet. Maybe it was the call of the blood of his mother's people, a call which he knew would lead to difficulties among the officers' clique and their wives in the Army where his career lay. Yet, despite these obstacles, he knew he would never know true happiness unless he won Evening Star.

Back among the girls and squaws, Evening Star rode her pinto pony with two travois poles lashed to its sides and a skinning knife at her belt. Her thoughts were troubled about Crazy Horse and Cas. Crazy Horse would have been her choice for a husband, providing he could give enough guns, bullets and horses to satisfy her father, Chief Spotted Tail. But she was strongly attracted to Cas in a different way. She remembered the good times when they had ridden together when she was small. She could remember his gentleness and his giving her the most prized possession she held, the hide of the white buffalo. She had no way of knowing that the decision would not be up to her. The decision would be made by Ynke-lo, the Lakota god of death.

CHAPTER SIX

Three buffalo scouts raced back to report that the great buffalo herd was in the valley beyond the next ridge. Chief Spotted Tail divided the hunters into two groups of one hundred and fifty each and sent one group to the northeast and the other to the southeast to circle the herd at a distance to prevent it from stampeding before the attack. Caspar rode with Crazy Horse, He Dog and Lone Bear. Little Big Man was so unpopular that neither hunting party wanted him along. Spotted Tail relegated him to join the rear guard warriors to protect the squaws and girls from attacks by raiding parties of Crows of Shoshones.

When Caspar's hunting party rode out of the aspens, High Backbone, the strong warrior who was in charge, made the soft call of the mountain quail. Instantly all the hunters dismounted and clapped a hand over the nostrils of their horses, for scarcely four hundred yards away thousands of buffalo were snuffing at the short buffalo grass, while the old bulls stood guard, their small, short-sighted eyes partially hidden by shaggy hair, their nostrils keening the wind for possible danger.

High Backbone took a small mirror from his medicine pouch and flashed it three times across the valley. Shortly, three answering flashes came from the far side of the valley.

'*Hoppo-up*,' High Backbone commanded, and all the hunters swung onto their horses. Dark eyes flashed with excitement as hunting arrows were notchd to bowstrings. A quick arm signal from High Backbone and the hunters moved on the herd at a gallop strung out in a long line facing the herd. Cries of, '*Hokahey! Hokahey!*' mingled with the drumming of unshod hoofs.

The old bulls, guarding the great herd, lifted their shaggy heads sharply, snorted, scented the man-enemies and started the herd milling as the Oglala hunters closed on the brown, shaggy mass from the northeast and southeast, passing up the old bulls in favor of the fat calves and cows.

Wild *yihoos* accompanied each kill. The smell of blood mingled with boiling dust clouds as the great herd stampeded toward the west, the hunters racing their ponies along the edges, making their kills. The Oglala hunters rode with one leg hooked through the war rope, enabling them to lean far over on the other side of their ponies and fire their arrows into the softness behind the front shoulder of the buffalo from a distance of three to four feet. Caspar, riding an army saddle was at a disadvantage. It took him three arrows to bring down his first kill from the saddle of his big appaloosa. Yet during the wild, dust-clouded stampede, Caspar brought down one young bull, two fat cows, and three calves. In tallying the score, kill credits were easily determined as each hunter had special markings on his arrows.

Meanwhile, the squaws, girls, and young boys had moved in on the hundreds of carcasses strewn along the valley floor, their sharp skinning knives busy removing the precious buffalo hides, and cutting the meat into sections for packing on the travois to be brought into camp. Particular care was taken to preserve the main intestines which would be washed and used to be packed with *pemmican*, a mixture of chopped meat, berries, and nuts which would stay preserved for months.

Caspar discovered Evening Star up to her

elbows in blood as she worked on a carcass with a fifteen-year-old boy. His first reaction as a West Pointer was one of revulsion, then the Indian heritage from his mother, Pretty Valley, took over and he accepted what he saw as the natural and only way of life for the Lakotas.

As he dismounted and walked over, Evening Star cut a tasty piece of warm liver and gave it to the boy, then took one for herself. When she saw Caspar, she smiled and offered him a piece of liver on her skinning knife. Caspar swallowed it and found it good.

'Did Cas kill many buffalo?' she asked.

'Cas killed only six. It is ten years since he used the bow and the arrow.'

'When the big snow comes, the lodges of the Oglalas will be warm. There will be plenty to eat. Cas would find them much better than the Soldier Fort.'

Crazy Horse, Lone Bear and He Dog rode up. Crazy Horse said, '*Hohahey*, Cas, the skinning and cutting is for the women and boys. Come with us for a quick swim in the river and then we will eat.'

'Evening Star will cook fresh buffalo hump for Cas and Crazy Horse. That also is woman's work,' she smiled meaningfully at Crazy Horse. Caspar swung onto his appaloosa.

'Soon Cas will tell Evening Star what work he would expect from a woman,' he grinned at her and rode off.

A crescent moon hung in the sky, lighting the slope where four Lakota warriors rode slowly around the pony herd, guarding against a sudden raid by their traditional enemies, the Crows, the Shoshones and the Snakes.

The Oglalas were camped on a bench above the river. Smoke from many fires drifted on the night air, carrying with it the acrid stench of piles of fresh buffalo hides, of drying meat and bones, mingled with the fragrance of pine and cedar. The hunting had been good. The Oglalas would fare well through the long winter months ahead, with plenty of smoked meat, pemmican and many more warm buffalo robes to keep out the bitter cold.

Caspar sat on his gray army blankets near a cookfire. As this was purely a buffalo hunt, no lodges had been brought along. The travois were to be used solely for bringing back buffalo hides and meat. Later, Caspar would roll in his blankets and sleep in the open, as would everyone else.

He had returned from swimming in the river in time to see Evening Star bring in her travois loaded with meat and buffalo hides. Her arms, breasts and upper torso were smeared with dried blood. She looked wild, barbaric, beautiful.

'*Hoye*. Evening Star brings much meat to the smoke fires. Then she will cleanse herself in the river so the Soldier Coat will not be ashamed of her.'

'Cas could never be ashamed of Evening Star,' he called back. Her teeth flashed a smile as she rode past.

Now Caspar sat on his blankets watching her working at the cookfire with Deep Waters and Brown Otter, her hair glistening in the firelight, loosely braided and still wet from the river. She was wearing a buckskin smock against the evening mist chill.

Others with Caspar in the circle near the cookfire, talking and smoking, were Crazy Horse, Lone Bear, He Dog, Chief Spotted Tail and his guest Gray Wolf of the Northern Cheyennes, a strong warrior noted for his unrelenting hostility toward all whites. The bearclaw necklace on his broad chest failed to hide the many scars of old wounds and the rawhide rips from making the sundance ritual.

Also sitting in the circle was Little Big Man, still angry because he had been ordered to the rear guard instead of joining the buffalo hunt. He sat next to Gray Wolf, his smoldering gaze directed across the small circle at Caspar, who he blamed for taking his place with the buffalo hunters rather than because of his own unpopularity with the Oglala tribe.

Evening Star turned from the cookfire with a large platter made of woven willows piled with big juicy chunks of buffalo hump. She offered the meat first to her father, Chief Spotted Tail, next to Gray Wolf because he was not only a famous warrior but also a guest, and then, as Little Big Man reached to help himself, she turned away and offered the meat to Caspar.

'The eyes of Evening Star must be blind that they did not see Little Big Man!' Little Big Man snarled.

Evening Star ignored the outburst and served Crazy Horse.

Not so with He Dog. '*Hou! Hou!*' he hooted. 'Even Little Big Man should know that the buffalo hunters are always fed first!'

'Buffalo hunters!' Little Big Man jeered. 'How many buffalo did Cas kill?'

Caspar grasped his large chunk of buffalo hump in his teeth and held five fingers of one hand and one finger of the other. Then he removed the meat from his mouth and answered, 'In case Little Big Man can't count, Cas killed six buffalo.'

'If Little Big Man had hunted instead of Cas, he would have killed ten, maybe eleven!' Little Big Man boasted.

'Cas made a strong showing,' Crazy Horse admonished. 'For it has been many snows since he hunted with the bow and arrow! Deep Waters, give Little Big Man some meat. It will stop the bad words in his mouth!'

Deep Waters carried some meat to Little

Big Man, who tore into it ravenously, his angry eyes still fixed on Caspar.

Chief Spotted Tail wiped his hands on his deerskin leggins, then filled his stone pipe with red willow bark. Evening Star brought him a flaming brand from the cookfire. When his pipe was drawing well, he turned to his Cheyenne guest and said, 'Gray Wolf, when you go home to Sand Creek, tell Chief Black Kettle that he is foolish to stay so near the Soldier Fort. Pretty quick many of his young women will move into the Woman's Camp to serve the Soldier Coats and his warriors will become lazy loaf-about-the-fort Indians and no longer warriors. Tell him to bring his Cheyennes up here where they will live free and where the buffalo, the elk and the deer have not yet walked away.'

'Your words are wise words,' Gray Wolf replied. 'But the ears of Chief Black Kettle listen only to the words of the agentfather, who tells him that if the Cheyennes remain on Sand Creek, the Riding Soldiers and the Walkaheaps will leave them in peace!'

'Peace! White man's peace!' Little Big Man spat vehemently. 'We were at peace on the Shell River and again on the Blue Water, and each time the Soldier Coats came to kill us!'

He pointed an accusing finger at Caspar. 'Cas comes here as our friend. But he is not our friend! He comes to spy on our strength and our weapons! Pretty quick he will lead

62

his Soldier Coats against us!'

Chief Spotted Tail rose quickly. His voice came sharp with anger. 'Hear me, Little Big Man! Cas is our guest. To insult a guest is to break a sacred law of the Lakotas.'

He picked up a bone whistle hanging from a rawhide string around his neck and blew three quick blasts. Immediately, four stalwart warriors arrived on the run. They were members of the *akacita*, the Lakota police. To them he said, 'Spotted Tail has closed the lodge doors of the Lakotas against Little Big Man! See that he gathers up his ponies and rides away. Now!'

Strong arms clamped down on the arms of Little Big Man. As he was led away he called back maliciously, 'Little Big Man will make new friends! He will become a scout for the Soldier Coats!'

Chief Spotted Tail stared grimly after Little Big Man, then resumed his seat and turned to Caspar. He said, 'Cas must name what presents he wants to make him forget this bad thing.'

Crazy Horse answered for Caspar, first touching the tips of the fingers on his left hand to his forehead in the Lakota sign of great respect. 'Long ago Cas knew that Little Big Man was a troublemaker. He will not need any presents to make him forget his bad words.'

Spotted Tail nodded approval. He said to

Cas, 'The blood of the Oglalas is in your heart, and so you know that some of Little Big Man's words were true words.'

Caspar touched the tips of the fingers of his left hand to his forehead before replying. He said, 'Cas saw Wyuse wound Conquering Bear. He saw the wagon-guns shoot through the lodges of the Brule-Lakotas.'

The eyes of Gray Wolf narrowed suspiciously.

Spotted Tail continued, his voice gentle. 'We know that the father of Cas is a Soldier Coat Chief and that it is an honorable thing to follow in the moccasin tracks of your father. Yet, Cas saw these bad things done to the Lakotas, so how can Cas still wear a Soldier Coat? Spotted Tail asks this not in anger, but as a friend.'

The eyes of Evening Star were on Caspar, wondering what his answer would be. Caspar dipped his head in thought for a moment, then spoke directly to Spotted Tail. He said, 'There have been many brutal killings of Lakotas and their Cheyenne cousins by the Soldier Coats and by the whites who mine for gold. These killings made their blood hot for revenge and they retaliated with more killings. And so Washington sent more Soldier Coats to fight the Lakotas and Cheyennes.' He shook his head. 'To stop these bad things was one strong reason why Cas now wears the Soldier Coat. He knows that if the heart of a Soldier Chief feels good toward the Lakotas and the Cheyennes, he will not talk to them with bullets and wagon-guns. Instead, he will come as a friend. Both sides will talk and whatever bad things that were between them will walk away and the peace will not be broken.'

Spotted Tail became thoughtful. Evening Star was both impressed and proud. Not so Crazy Horse. He said, with a faint smile, '*Hou*! That will be a very big thing to see.'

This made Caspar realize that while he was his friend, Crazy Horse placed no trust in the United States Army.

Later, when Spotted Tail and others were asleep, wrapped in their blankets, Caspar, Crazy Horse and Evening Star sat near the dying embers of the cookfire, their blankets over their shoulders against the night chill from the river.

Caspar smoked his pipe silently, staring into the dying fire. Crazy Horse made a tiny whistling noise as he smoked his little stone pipe. Presently he shook his head, tapped out the ashes from his pipe and said, 'No, Cas, talk of a lasting peace would only be a trap for the Lakotas. For pretty quick the whites would want more of our land and the Soldier Coats would come against us to take it.'

Caspar glanced at Evening Star and found her staring off at the moonlit hills. He said, 'Does Evening Star believe in what Crazy

Horse has said?'

She spoke slowly, prophetically. 'Only Wana Tanka knows where the moccasin trail will lead us. But Evening Star believes that one day Cas will find this peace thing.'

Crazy Horse said quietly, 'Ever since Cas gave her the white buffalo hide she has told of many strange things that became true.'

Caspar saw that Crazy Horse was serious and he glanced at Evening Star. Her eyes were sad and caught the moonlight as she stared as in a trance at the distant hills. He knew he had never seen a woman more beautiful.

CHAPTER SEVEN

On the crest of a nearby hill, two Crow scouts lay, bellied down, watching the guards riding slowly around the pony herd and six *akacitas* guarding the sleeping camp below. Their faces were painted for war and both were armed with a war club, a bow and a quiver of arrows, their dark bodies naked but for breechcloths and moccasins. Each wore a lone eagle feather in his hair, signifying he had killed his man and had achieved warrior status. For a while they studied the camp, watching the *akacitas* occasionally feed wood to the smoke fires. Then one Crow scout made a quick hand signal to the other and both wriggled backwards to disappear over the crest of the hill.

At first sunup, the Oglala camp became a beehive of activity. The squaws were busy freshening the smoke fires, turning the long strips of buffalo meat and bone scraping the inner sides of the buffalo hides. Many of the young women and boys had gone up the hill to bring down the pony herd to water it in the river.

Caspar threw his McClellan saddle on his appaloosa and tightened the cinch. On his blankets nearby were his bow, quiver of arrows and his Springfield carbine, a cartridge belt with metal cartridges in loops and button-down holster, enclosing a Smith and Wesson six—shot revolver, also his shirt, tunic, and campaign hat.

Close by, Crazy Horse was adjusting the hackamore and war rope on his buckskin.

Evening Star, Deep Waters and Brown Otter rode by herding some ponies toward the river, clad only in breechcloths and moccasins. Evening Star pulled her pony over to Caspar. She smiled and said, '*Hohahe*, Cas. Evening Star will water Cas's pony for him.'

'Thanks. Cas is going to water his horse and take a swim, too. But he is going to swim upstream, where the water won't taste pony,' he grinned.

'Pretty quick Evening Star will join Cas for

a swim,' she cried gaily as she rode on.

Caspar grinned then threw her a casual salute. Crazy Horse frowned momentarily. He was not happy to find Evening Star making such overt advances to his friend Cas.

Caspar picked up his cartridge belt and attached revolver holster and hung it over the cantle of his McClellen saddle and mounted.

Crazy Horse asked derisively, 'Cas needs his revolver to go swimming with Evening Star. Why is this?'

'For rattlesnakes and jealous Lakota friends,' Caspar grinned. 'Cas saw a big diamondback on the river bank when he returned from the hunt yesterday.'

He rode off, angling down slope for a point upstream. As he rode he saw Evening Star, Deep Waters and Brown Otter herd their ponies into the water to the middle of the shallows. Hidden by the willows and cottonwoods on the far side of the river sat the Crow raiding party, fifteen in number, watching the girls watering the Lakota ponies in the midstream shallows.

Two of the Crows were armed with rifles, the others with lances, bows and arrows. Four of them held rawhide lassos, coiled and ready for action. Laughter from the girls in the river rose up to them. Dark eyes glittered with anticipation. The leader, a stalwart young warrior in his midtwenties who was one of the lasso holders, said, 'The girl on the pinto is mine!' He gave a quick hand signal and the raiding party lunged forward.

The first inkling Evening Star had of trouble was when Brown Otter suddenly screamed, '*AAAAAAAH!*' the Lakota warning of danger. She turned her head quickly and heeled her pony with the same motion. But she was not fast enough. The rawhide lasso of the Crow leader dropped over her shoulders, the noose jerked tight, pinning her bare arms to her sides and she was yanked from her pinto into the river. Then a powerful dark hand fastened onto her long hair and she was lifted, kicking and biting, onto the Crow leader's lap. A sharp, cruel blow to the base of her skull, delivered from the side of his stiff hand and Evening Star lost consciousness. Deep Waters and Brown Otter were similarly dealt with, but not before their warning cries had alerted the whole Lakota camp.

Caspar was loping along the sloping bench to his upstream swim when Brown Otter's first cry of warning reached him. When other cries came from the girls, he whirled his big appaloosa and put it at a gallop for the danger area, snatching his revolver belt from the saddle cantle and buckling it around his waist. He flipped open the holster cover, making his six-shot Smith and Wesson free for action.

He put his mount into the river ford in

time to see the Crow leader reach the far bank with Evening Star's inert body slung across his knees. Close behind him were other Crows carrying Deep Waters and Brown Otter. Caspar was not yet close enough to risk a shot without danger of hurting one of the captured girls.

Meanwhile, the Lakota warriors had snatched up weapons and mounts. Some of them ran into the stream to leap on the back of a pony that was being watered. Leading the warriors was Crazy Horse on his buckskin, shouting the Lakota war cry, 'Hokahey! Hokahey!' He was closely followed by He Dog and Lone Bear.

On the far bank, the Crows were howling insults as they let drive their arrows at Caspar and the nearest infuriated Lakotas. Caspar flattened low in the saddle. One arrow stuck quivering in the cantle. The Crow who fired it urged his pony forward for a closer shot at Caspar. Caspar's bullet took him in the chest and he tumbled from his pony. One Lakota took an arrow in the throat, then Crazy Horse and his Lakotas sent their arrows thrumming at the Crows. Two dropped, the rest wheeled their ponies and fled.

Caspar, Crazy Horse and the van of the Lakotas thundered after the Crows as they sought to escape through the sparsely wooded slope, heading for a long stretch of pine forest cresting the slope. Crazy Horse, one leg hooked under his war rope, leaned far down on the offside of his buckskin, raced alongside a fleeing Crow and, from below the buckskin's neck, drove an arrow into the Crow's side. The Crow warrior screeched and fell from his pony. Instantly, Crazy Horse leapt from the buckskin, whipping out his scalping knife.

A high-pitch howl from the Crow leader made the raiders scatter like a covey of quail. The Lakotas, splitting into smaller hunting parties, howled after them.

Caspar saw the Crow leader cut off toward the western end of the pine forest, with the unconscious form of Evening Star still slung across his lap. He was accompanied by another warrior. Caspar raced after them, his big appaloosa rapidly gaining on the pair. The second Crow threw a quick glance back over his shoulder and saw that Caspar was overtaking them fast and would soon be in effective revolver range. Applying his wrist whip harder, he forged ahead of his leader, using him as a shield.

When Caspar closed within good revolver range of the Crow leader, Evening Star regained consciousness and, though still tightly bound by the rawhide lasso, she started struggling again. The Crow leader cast a quick glance at Caspar, then grasped Evening Star by her thick hair, bent low and tossed her over his back for protection.

71

Pursued and pursuer raced into the pine forest.

When the pines became dense enough to slow escape, the leading Crow leapt from his pony, notched an arrow to his bowstring. Before he could let drive at Caspar, the latter's bullet smashed him between the eyes. His death yell echoed through the trees. Caspar pulled up, listening. Hearing no hoof beats from the Crow leader, he dismounted and advanced cautiously, his revolver ready.

Meanwhile, the Crow leader had hurled Evening Star roughly to the ground, partially stunning her, dismounted and took cover behind some tall ferns at the base of a tree. When he saw Caspar coming in his direction, he picked up a large pine cone and threw it to the right.

Caspar heard the sound of the fallen pine cone and instantly froze, then cautiously started to move toward the sound. From nearby ferns Evening Star called a muffled warning and instantly Caspar started to change direction, dropping into a crouch. This action saved his life, for the Crow leader's arrow slammed into his left shoulder. The shock of the impact dropped Caspar to his knees and the Crow leader leapt forward, his war club raised for the kill. From a kneeling position, Caspar drove two bullets into his chest. Because the bullets traversed upwards, one must have ripped through the

Crow leader's heart, for his knees buckled. His death cry was cut off by the death rattle. He collapsed a foot from where Caspar knelt. His sinewy body twitched, then was still.

Caspar lurched to his feet and ran over to where Evening Star lay, frantically calling her name as she tried to free her arms from the tight loops of the rawhide lasso. There was a scrape on one cheekbone, caused when the Crow leader had hurled her roughly to the ground. She lay on her side, her back to Caspar as he dropped to his knee beside her. She did not see the Crow arrow in his shoulder.

'Are you hurt,' Caspar asked, anxiously, working with both hands to free her, despite the acute pain from his wounded shoulder.

Evening Star shook her head. 'More angry than hurt,' she panted. 'But her heart was torn with fear that Cas would be killed.'

'Cas would have been killed, but for your warning cry,' he said, as he succeeded in loosening the rawhide lasso. She sat up, rubbing her arms, then suddenly she saw the feathered arrow shaft protruding from Caspar's upper left chest.

'Cas! Cas has been hurt,' she cried. She sprang to her feet, anxiously examining the wound. Caspar's anger rose as he saw inflamed red marks across her body and lovely breasts, left by the rawhide noose. Then he felt her fingers gently probing his

73

upper back.

'Too bad the barb didn't go right through,' he said. 'Ouch! That's it.'

'The barbed point is just beneath the skin. Evening Star will have to push it through!'

'Go ahead. And, I shall call you Star. Evening Star is too big a mouthful for use between us.' He picked up a loop of the rawhide noose and clamped his teeth down on it.

He sat down. Evening Star knelt in front of him. She placed one knee between his legs, put an arm around his back, pressing her silken body against him.

'Evening Star will be most careful. But the barb must come through far enough for Evening Star to get a big hold on it.'

She felt the point of the barb beneath the skin of his back, then spread her fingers, pressing around it. Then, with her right hand on the arrow shaft and the weight of her shoulder behind it, she put pressure on it. Sweat appeared on Caspar's forehead but, teeth firmly clamped down on the rawhide, he emitted no sound.

The pointed barb of the arrow made exit between Evening Star's pressing fingers. When the shaft protruded about six inches, she stopped the pressure, gave Caspar an anxious, searching look and said, 'Now Star needs a knife!'

She ran quickly to the body of the dead

Crow leader, pulled the hunting knife from his beaded, deerskin belt, returned to Caspar and expertly cut the arrow shaft off close to the point of entry. Next, she caught hold of the protruding barbed shaft and, pressing her fingers on either side of the wound, began gently easing it out.

The severed end of the arrow shaft disappeared inside Caspar's chest and a trickle of blood appeared. But, when Evening Star eased the barbed shaft from Caspar's back, blood spurted out. 'Cas,' she cried in alarm, 'It is bleeding big!'

'Let it bleed,' Cas gritted. 'May take any poison out.'

'Deermoss will draw out the poison better,' Evening Star exclaimed. She ran off into the forest. Caspar flexed his wounded shoulder, winced, then proceeded to eject the used metal cartridges from his Smith and Wesson and to replace the empties with fresh cartridges from his belt, in case of further trouble with the Crow raiders, although this seemed unlikely as the war whoops of the Lakotas and howling of the Crows were fast fading in the distance.

Evening Star ran back from the forest with an arm full of deermoss. This she deposited on the ground beside Caspar. Then she stripped the beaded deerskin belt from the dead Crow. Next, she carefully placed a wadded bunch of deermoss on Caspar's bleeding back wound, and over it the deerskin belt.

'Soon the pain will walk away. Now Cas must lie down on his back, so the deermoss can stop the bleeding and draw out the poison.'

'Begins to feel easier already,' Cas said. He did as he was told. Then she put another deermoss poultice on the front wound and tied it in place with the ends of the deerskin belt. As she was doing this, her lovely, full left breast, with its swollen aureola was only inches from Caspar's face and he could not resist caressing it with his right hand. She did not pull away. She merely gave him a puzzled glance and said, 'Why does Cas do this strange thing?'

Caspar was well aware that both Lakota and Cheyenne males had no interest in their women's breasts, other than their use in suckling their children. Neither did the husband and wife indulge in love play. When a warrior lusted, he simply took his woman when the urge moved him. Apart from that, a woman's role was relegated to bearing and raising children, cooking, making moccasins and all other camp chores. The warriors confined their activities solely to tribal councils, where women were not allowed, to hunting and to protecting the women, children and old ones from all enemies, both white and red.

Caspar knew that all these old traditions were deeply ingrained in this wild, lovely girl of his choice. Yet, he felt it might not be too difficult to teach her some of the good things that were important to the white man.

He said, 'Hear me, Star. To the Soldier Coats, and the other whites, the breasts of a woman have big meaning. Some they consider to be beautiful. Yours are very beautiful. They like to fondle and kiss them, like this.' He brushed his lips lightly over the mound of her left breast and felt the instant response of her nipple. She caught her breath, but she did not pull back from him.

'When a Soldier Coat chooses a woman, he insists she keep her breasts covered from all other eyes but his own,' he continued. 'The word love has no meaning among the Lakotas. But to the Soldier Coats love has big meaning. He and his woman become as one. They hold no secrets from each other. When he is out on patrol, above everything else, he looks forward to coming home to her, to the nights when he can sleep, holding her soft warmth in his arms. Does Star understand what Cas is saying?'

She regarded him gravely. Her wide eyes were dark and mysterious. 'Does Cas mean that he wants Star for his wife?' she asked.

'Yes,' Caspar said. 'Cas wants Star for his wife.'

'Does Cas also mean that Star would have

to leave the Lakotas and go to live in the Soldier Fort?'

Caspar nodded. 'My mother, Pretty Valley, left the lodges of the Lakotas to live in the Soldier Fort with my father. She was very happy because he loved her dearly. Now, before I ask your father, Chief Spotted Tail, what presents I must give him, I must ask Star if she feels this love for Cas?'

Evening Star's eyes became sad, troubled.

'Is there someone else? Crazy Horse perhaps?' he asked.

'The heart of Star is split between Crazy Horse and Cas,' she said, unhappily.

A twig snapped close by. Instantly, Caspar's hand went to his revolver, only to relax as Crazy Horse joined them. Crazy Horse stood looking down at them, his face inscrutable. Three fresh scalps dangled from his belt.

'Cas killed two Crows,' Evening Star told him proudly. 'He is a strong warrior!'

'So none of the Crow war party lives to tell their people how they died,' he commented vengefully.

He sent a long call echoing through the forest. Then he dropped to one knee and gently examined Caspar's wound, front and back.

'Evening Star got the arrow out,' Caspar told him. Crazy Horse nodded approval and said gravely, 'Five fingers lower and the heart

78

of Evening Star would no longer be split between us.'

Caspar caught the edge to Crazy Horse's voice. Yet the hands on his shoulders remained gentle. Caspar grinned, nodded, 'It was close. The spirit of Cas almost walked away.'

A faint smile touched the lips of Crazy Horse. He said, 'The life of a close friend is a bigger thing than winning a wife.'

Evening Star gave a sigh of relief, happy that the friendship was still intact and feeling no sense of having been slighted. Lakota victory howls and the drumming of hoofs from the forest announced He Dog and Lone Bear coming in response to Crazy Horse's calls. Crazy Horse threw back his head and called back, '*Eeyah! Eeeyah!* Over here!'

Shortly, He Dog and Lone Bear appeared, weaving fast among the pines. They circled the fight area, then drew rein beside their friends.

Lone Bear exulted, '*Hou!* Now all the Crows are dead!'

He Dog, his sense of propriety outraged, cried out indignantly, 'Cas! These two Crows still wear their scalps! Why is this?'

Caspar laughed and said, 'Cas gives them to his old friends He Dog and Lone Bear.'

Grinning broadly, both warriors leapt from their ponies and whipped out their scalping knives.

CHAPTER EIGHT

At sunset, Caspar came riding down out of the hills, his right arm in a rawhide sling. Below he could see Fort Laramie beside the North Platte River. The light breeze carried the trumpet notes of 'Retreat,' and on the broad parade ground he could see the flag being lowered.

Evening Star, Crazy Horse, He Dog and Lone Bear had accompanied him as far as the Belle Fourche. At their leaving, Crazy Horse, He Dog and Lone Bear had turned back first, allowing Evening Star a few moments alone with Caspar.

'Did Crazy Horse plan for us to be alone?' he asked. She shook her head. 'It was Star,' she replied with a faint smile.

Caspar had not managed to be alone with Evening Star since he was wounded. Crazy Horse had kept him in his own lodge where his wound was attended by his sister. It had seemed to Caspar that Evening Star had purposely avoided being alone with him.

He said, 'Why has Star not walked alone with Cas since he was wounded?'

She regarded him thoughtfully a moment, then replied, 'To leave the lodges of the Lakotas and go to the Soldier Fort would be a very big change. Yet Star keeps giving much thought to this love thing Cas told her about.'

'Does Star mean that she has decided to become the wife of Cas?' he asked hopefully.

'Cas saved Star from becoming a slave of the Crows, so her life belongs to him,' she said softly.

Caspar frowned, shaking his head, 'Cas does not want Star because she feels she owes him a debt. He wants her because she feels love for him.'

'Cas must hurry back to the lodges of the Lakotas.' She gave him a flashing smile, turned her pinto pony and loped after her companions.

Caspar recreated their parting in his mind as he rode toward the fort. He was smiling because he felt he was going to win Star for his wife.

At the fort gates Caspar took the salute from the sentry. As he cantered across the parade ground, lights were springing up along Officers' Row, in the enlisted men's barracks and the sutler's store.

He dismounted at the stables and turned the big appaloosa over to his striker. The man's eyes strayed questioningly to the rawhide sling on Caspar's right arm but asked no questions.

'Water Lakota and give him plenty of oats. He's been two weeks without his oats rations,' Caspar ordered.

'I'll take good care of Lakota, Lieutenant,'

the striker said. Caspar walked around Lakota, gave him an affectionate pat on the rump and, with his right hand, pulled his carbine from the saddleboot.

Captain Fetterman, accompanied by Lieutenant Ransome and Sergeant Hanna, came out of the stables, having just finished stables inspection. All came to an abrupt halt. Captain Fetterman and Lieutenant Ransome eyed Caspar's sling with mild amusement, Sergeant Hanna with concern.

'I see that your friends, the Sioux, had the welcome mat out, Mr. Collins,' Captain Fetterman remarked sardonically.

'How about the hair, Caspar,' Lieutenant Ransome grinned maliciously. 'Did the Sioux lift that, too?'

Caspar suddenly tossed his carbine at Lieutenant Ransome, who, though taken by surprise, caught it expertly. Then Caspar made them both a facetious bow and removed his campaign hat, proving that his full head of hair was still intact.

'The Lakotas tangled with a Crow war party, I managed to stop an arrow,' he informed them.

Sergeant Hanna said, 'I saw Dr. Lunt go into his hospital half an hour ago. Maybe the Lieutenant should have him check the wound for infection?'

Caspar nodded. 'I'll have him change the bandages, Mike. But there's no infection. A

Lakota girl took good care of me.' He retrieved his carbine from Lieutenant Ransome, adding evenly, 'She was a real beauty, George.'

That evening Caspar went to his father's quarters and sat with his father and Victoria before the fire, talking. He had Dr. Lunt, the contract surgeon, check his wound. He pronounced it free of infection and put on fresh bandages and a regular sling to replace the rawhide one. During supper in the Officers' Mess, he had been subjected to a certain amount of ribbing, instigated largely by Lieutenant Ransome and, but for the latter's contribution, it had all been good-natured.

Victoria and the major listened with keen interest to Caspar's account of the buffalo hunt. When he had finished, the major said, 'Six buffalo with bow and arrow. I'd call that pretty fair shooting, Caspar. I remember back in 1840, at old Fort McPherson, I was a second lieutenant at the time, I tried my hand at the bow and arrow. We'd set up a target on the stable doors of H Troop,' he chuckled, shaking his head. 'My first arrow not only missed the target, it missed the entire stable, sailed over the roof and through the open upstairs bedroom window of the colonel's quarters and stuck slapdab in a large, framed photograph of his mother-in-law.'

'So that's why it took you so long to make

first lieutenant, Rufus,' Victoria laughed. 'I've often wondered about that.'

'Nooo,' the major grinned. 'Matter of fact, my promotion came through shortly after. I've always suspected the colonel appreciated the quality of my marksmanship.'

When the laughter died down, Major Collins became serious. He said, 'Tell me about this scrap with the Crows, Caspar. Because if they're out looking for trouble the Army may have to take action.'

'The Lakotas saved the Army the expense of any action, Dad,' Caspar rejoined. 'The entire Crow war party ended up being very dead.' He grinned and touched a match to his pipe.

'Don't you dare stop now, Caspar,' Victoria exclaimed, smiling. 'Rufus, don't allow him to leave me sitting on the edge of my chair.'

'Go ahead, Caspar. Give Vic all the gory details.'

'It happened shortly after sunup the morning after the buffalo hunt,' Caspar began. 'Some of the older boys and girls were watering the pony herd in the shallows of the Rosebud River. The Crow war party was hiding in the willows and cottonwoods across the river. The war party numbered fifteen, mostly young bucks. They were out to capture some Lakota girls. The shrill warning cries of the girls alerted the camp and we streaked into the river after them, but not

84

before three of the girls had been lassoed. One of the girls was Evening Star, the daughter of Chief Spotted Tail—you remember her, Dad—ten years ago she was known as Little Singing Stream.

The major nodded. 'Pretty as a picture and she could ride like the wind, too. Yes, I remember her.'

The major followed Caspar's account of the fight with a soldier's interest. Victoria, on the other hand, was mostly interested in the Indian girl Caspar referred to as Star. She noticed his expression change when he mentioned her name, the pride in his voice. She also sensed something else, something which gave her vague misgivings.

'That's about it,' Caspar concluded. 'Star had the arrow out of my shoulder and had it bandaged when Crazy Horse rode up to tell us the fight was over. Casualties were fifteen Crows dead, one Lakota killed and three and a half Lakota wounded. The half Lakota being me.'

'Hmph!' ejaculated Major Collins, approvingly. 'I'd say that established some sort of a record for fast retaliation to a surprise attack. Who led it? Chief Spotted Tail?'

'Gosh, I don't know, Dad,' Caspar shook his head. 'I was mounted and closest to the river when the Crows hit. I saw the Crow leader capture Star and I simply took off after him. I guess it was just a case of each Lakota picking his own Crow.' He tossed a grin at his father, who chuckled in return.

Victoria said, slowly, 'Caspar, your father said that when he saw Little Singing Stream ten years ago, she was very pretty. Is—is she still very pretty?'

'No, Vic, Star isn't just very pretty, she's downright gorgeous! She would make a wife a man'd be proud of anywhere!'

Victoria caught her breath, shot an alarmed look at her husband.

'Caspar, you—you aren't seriously thinking of—?' the major said quietly.

'Yes, I am, Dad. I've already asked Star to become my wife. But I've got competition for her—Crazy Horse. However, I do have one advantage over Crazy Horse.'

'And that is?' his father prodded.

'As you know, Dad, the word love has no meaning to the Lakotas. I've explained the meaning to Star. She knows that I'm in love with her.'

This was a delicate subject to bring up before Victoria, although, in a way, she was responsible for bringing it up. Ever since she met Major Collins, she had closed her mind to the fact that his first wife was a full-blooded Oglala-Lakota woman. She rose and said, 'I—I think you two will feel more at ease if I leave you alone.' She put an affectionate hand on Caspar's shoulder and kissed his cheek. 'Good night, Caspar. Remember, your father and I only want what will be best for you.' With a soft rustle of silk she was gone.

Caspar took a deep breath and exhaled. 'Sorry, Dad. I didn't mean to say anything to offend Vic.'

Major Collins shook his head as he tapped the doffle from his pipe. 'No, you didn't offend Vic, son. Vic was born on an army post, like you. She was an army brat. But, unlike you, she was born and raised back East where the Officer's Code was pretty rigid, and still is. Vic's only concern is for your career, son.'

Caspar frowned and busied himself filling and lighting his pipe. Both men stared into the fire silently for a while, each preoccupied with his own thoughts, Caspar with his determined thoughts of Star and the major with his nostalgic memories of Caspar's Oglala mother, Pretty Valley.

Presently, the major leaned back in his chair, blew a smoke ring and watched it rise lazily toward the overhead pine beams. He said, 'I've never regretted marrying your mother, son, not for one moment.' He gave a deep sigh. 'But that happened about twenty-five years ago when white women found on the frontier that a man would want to marry were practically nonexistent, particularly if he had only the low army pay.

On the other hand, among the Lakotas and Cheyennes were many beautiful girls, their morals were very strict. If one of them cut her virgin's rope before marriage, she was thrown out of her village. Many officers and enlisted men married them. And the top brass simply looked the other way. Now things have changed and the top brass takes a rather harsh view of such alliances.'

Caspar's mouth tightened. 'Are you saying that if I married Star, I'd be asked to resign my commission?' he asked.

'No,' his father said slowly. 'At least, not formally. But, as your Lakota wife, Star would be ignored by the wives of your brother officers, and you'd draw duty on lonely frontier posts. And the chances for promotion would be very remote. That'd be the life for you and Star, if you chose to stick it out.'

Caspar rose, smiled. 'It was a long trek from the Oglala village. I think I'd better hit the hay.' He laid a hand on his father's shoulder. 'Thanks for worrying about me. Goodnight, Dad.'

The major looked up at his son, searchingly. 'Will you give some thought to what I've said, son? It's pretty important.'

'Once you see Star, Dad, you'll understand why I'm going to marry her, even if it means I'll someday become the oldest second lieutenant in the United States Army!

Goodnight, Dad.'

Major Collins remained, staring into the fire for a while before joining Victoria in their bedroom. He found her still awake. She greeted him with an anxious, questioning look in her wide, green eyes. He gave her a worried smile as he began to unbutton his tunic.

Her eyes became apprehensive. She said, 'Did you and Caspar get anything settled, Rufus?'

'I find that that young man has quite a mind of his own, Vic,' he replied, hanging up his tunic in the closet.

'But, he is an extremely handsome young man, Rufus. Surely, while at the Academy, he must have met many attractive girls at the dances at the Hotel Thayer.'

The major sat on the edge of the bed and began tugging at his field boots. 'Evidently, none of them could hold a candle to this Lakota girl.'

'You mean Caspar really intends to marry her?'

The major removed one field boot, and started working on the other. 'Yes, Vic, he does. If he can win her away from Crazy Horse, even though he is well aware that such a marriage will raise hob with his army career. Vic, I can't help feeling pretty proud of that young man.'

'Oh, you men.' Vic's eyes filled, but she

was smiling. 'You pick a star and you follow it blindly, consequences be hanged! I—I supposed that is why we women love you so much.'

He turned, took her in his arms and gently kissed her tears away. 'I think that Caspar has chosen his star, and you are a very wonderful woman, Vic,' he murmured.

Outside, in the bright moonlight the long, sad notes of 'Taps' ran the Parade.

CHAPTER NINE

Like all forts, life at Fort Laramie fell into the old, established routines of reveille, stables, mess, fatigue and drill calls, a monotony broken only by going out on patrol or by visits from high-ranking inspecting officers. This particular hot summer day promised to be no different from any other. The water wagon moved slowly along Officers' Row, sprinkling the dust. It would continue on past Headquarters, then return on a parellel course. Lieutenant Gourlay cantered out through the fort gates, leading a detail of B Troop on patrol.

Out on the Parade, Corporal Big Mouth was going through the motions of drilling his platoon of Indian scouts. Dust puffs rose as the Indians, unaccustomed to the heavy army boots, dragged their feet.

Caspar and Sergeant Hanna left the stables and started across the Parade for headquarters. Caspar still wore his right arm in a sling. Sergeant Hanna said, 'You had that shoulder checked by the contract surgeon lately, Lieutenant?'

'Ha,' Caspar laughed. 'You must use mental telepathy, Mike. Dr. Lunt grabbed me at mess this morning, took me over to his meat factory and gave me a thorough prodding. Said it was healing nicely and I could drop the sling next week. He just warned me to take it easy with my left shoulder.'

'Such as no chinning yourself on the stable doors, eh Lieutenant?' Sergeant Hanna prodded.

Caspar grinned, shook his head. They stopped their progress to allow Corporal Big Mouth and his platoon to pass. Sergeant Hanna viewed them sourly. He growled, 'They make good scouts, I'll allow, Lieutenant, but, b' jasus, as soldiers they'll never cut it.'

Caspar started to smile, then suddenly his smile vanished.

'Corporal, halt your platoon!' he yelled.

Corporal Big Mouth gave the order and his platoon came to a sloppy halt. As Caspar and Sergeant Hanna walked over, Corporal Big Mouth came to a salute.

'Something is bad, Lieutenant?' he asked.

'You're damn right something is bad,' he snapped, as his eyes fixed on the rear man of number-five file. He was staring into the leering face of Little Big Man. 'What the hell are you doing here?' he demanded.

'Little Big Man Soldier Coat now. Same like Cas,' the man replied, his malicious grin widening.

'Corporal,' Caspar ordered, 'Relieve this man of his rifle and sidearm and march him over to Headquarters.'

When Caspar entered Headquarters, he found Captain Fetterman with his father. He snapped to attention and saluted.

'I found Little Big Man drilling with the Scout Platoon. Did the major ask him why he chose to leave the lodges of the Lakotas?'

'No, I didn't, mister. I was glad to get him. Free Indians make much better scouts than the lazy loaf-about-the-fort Indians,' the major returned.

'I took the liberty of ordering Little Big Man brought in. His reason for leaving the lodges of the Lakotas might change your mind about him, sir.'

An orderly ushered in Sergeant Hanna, Corporal Big Mouth and Little Big Man. Sergeant Hanna came to a stiff salute and announced, 'Sergeant Hanna, Corporal Big Mouth and Recruit Little Big Man, reporting, sir!'

'At ease,' Major Collins said, returning the salute. 'Little Big Man, what were your reasons for leaving the lodges of the Lakotas?'

Little Big Man shot an angry glance at Caspar.

He said arrogantly, 'The Soldier Coats eat big, sleep warm. Heap better than in lodges of the Lakotas.'

'Mr Collins?' the major formally gave Caspar his chance for rebuttal.

'Sir,' Caspar answered, ignoring the glare from Little Big Man, 'Chief Spotted Tail closed the lodges of the Lakotas to Little Big Man because he was a troublemaker, because none of the warriors would hunt buffalo with him, and because he broke the sacred law of the Lakotas by insulting a guest, meaning myself. He ordered the *akacita* to see that Little Big Man gathered his ponies and rode away!'

'Sounds as if Little Big Man is exactly the type of scout we need, Major,' Captain Fetterman commented.

'Why do you say that, Captain?' the major asked.

'If the lodges of the Lakotas are closed to him, at least we'd know he's on our side,' the captain returned lightly, flicking an amused glance at Caspar. Caspar caught the double entendre, but his expression remained unchanged.

'I disagree, Captain,' the major rejoined,

crisply. 'This is no time to offer insult to Chief Spotted Tail and his Lakotas, which enlisting Little Big Man would be. Sergeant, take away Little Big Man's uniform, give him a week's rations and see him off the post!'

'Yes, sir!' Sergeant Hanna snapped.

Little Big Man's face filled with fury. He lashed out at Caspar. 'Little Big Man knows where to get another Soldier Coat! He will become a Soldier Coat Chief! A bigger Soldier Coat Chief than Cas!'

'Shut that big mouth! About turn!' Sergeant Hanna rasped. 'Forward march! One two three four.'

Half an hour later, Caspar and Sergeant Hanna stood on the steps of Headquarters and watched Little Big Man ride out, leading his other two ponies. Divested of his uniform, he was bare except for breechcloth, leggings and moccasins.

'There goes one dirty, stinking, dangerous polecat, Lieutenant,' Sergeant Hanna spat disgustedly into the dust.

Caspar nodded agreement and said, thoughtfully, 'I wonder where Little Big Man thinks he's going to get another Soldier Coat?'

* * *

Caspar sat on his big appaloosa, his saber at the present. He had long since discarded his arm sling. Behind him, Sergeant Hanna and a mounted detail also sat, sabers at the present. A trumpeter sounded 'Retreat' and a corporal lowered the flag.

When the corporal finished folding the flag, Caspar wheeled his mount to face his detail.

'Return sabers!' he ordered. Sabers rasped home into scabbards.

'Detail, prepare to dismount!'

Each trooper kicked his right boot free of the stirrup. Calloused right hands grasped the cantles of McClellan saddles. Left hands shortened their grip on the reins.

'Dismount!'

The troopers swung down. Stood to their horses.

'Dismissed!'

Caspar dismounted as his striker arrived on the double. A trumpet call sounded from Headquarters.

'Officers' Call, Lieutenant,' the striker exclaimed. 'And close to mess time, too. Wonder what's up.'

'There's one sure way to find out, trooper,' Caspar returned, as he started swiftly for Headquarters. Other officers left Officers' Row, moving quickly for the same destination.

Slouched in a chair near Major Collins' desk was Caleb Parker, a hulking, unprepossessing buffalo hide hunter. His face was bloated from hard drinking and his thick hair was centered with a wide white streak.

He was dressed in buckskins that were dirty, greasy and smoke blackened. The officers assembled quickly, standing rigidly at attention. Caspar felt an even stronger contempt for hide hunters, because they slaughtered buffalo indiscriminately, taking only the hides and leaving the meat to rot, meat that was badly needed among the lodges of the Lakotas and Cheyennes.

When all officers, except those on duty or out on patrol had assembled, Major Collins said, 'At ease, gentlemen. Gentlemen, this is Mr. Caleb Parker. He is a buffalo hide hunter. Tell them your story, Mr Parker.'

Caleb Parker chewed on his dead cigar butt, then leaned back in his chair, assuming an air of injured innocence. He said, 'Like I was telling the major here, about four days ago me an' my outfit located some buffalo. A small herd, but all were prime hides. We snuk up on 'em keeping downwind until we wuz close. Then we started shootin'. We knocked down about twenty-five of the varmints afore the herd spooked. Then we took off after 'em, running 'em fer about two miles and knockin' down some more.' He paused to relight his cigar, enjoying being the center of attention.

'Well, gents, we backtracked, peeling hides as we went an' pilin' hides fer the wagons to pick up later. When we got near where we made our first kill, we found the place

96

crawling with stinkin' Oglala-Sioux, bucks an' squaws skinnin' our buffalo!'

'How many men were in your outfit, Mr. Parker?' Captain Fetterman asked.

'Seven, includin' me, Cap'n,' Caleb Parker said.

'Seven of you. All armed with rifles and you let the Sioux bamboozle you out of your property?' Captain Fetterman chided.

'Whut? Us take on sixty-odd Oglala-Sioux? We warn't thet crazy, Cap'n. No sirree. We figgered you fellars'd ride into the Oglala camp an' make Chief Spotted Tail fork over them forty-odd prime buffalo hides!'

'With your permission, Major,' Captain Fetterman said, briskly, 'I'll take a troop up there and a howitzer. Those Oglalas'll hand over those hides or I'll crack into 'em!'

'And touch off a first-class Indian war,' Major Collins reprimanded. 'You are aware, Captain, that all commands have explicit orders to do their best to avoid hostilities with the Indians until this War between the States is over and reinforcements sent out?'

'Wouldn't mean any war, sir. I'd simply call their bluff.'

'For your information, Captain,' the major retorted, 'The Lakotas do not bluff. Neither do their cousins, the Cheyennes. We will handle this situation diplomatically.' He turned to Lieutenant Ransome. 'Mister, take a thirty-man detail from A Troop and investigate Mr. Parker's claim. Jim Bridger is away on leave, so Mr. Collins will go with you. I strongly suggest that you allow Mr. Collins to conduct all negotiations with Chief Spotted Tail!'

'Should be a nice, friendly visit, sir,' Lieutenant Ransome remarked, casually.

'Such is the purpose, mister. Any questions, Mr. Collins?'

'Sir,' said Caspar, 'I'd like to ask Mr. Parker the exact location where he and his men made their first kill.'

'Below Pumpkin Butte,' Caleb Parker squinted suspiciously. 'Bout six miles this side o' Powder River. Whassa difference, anyway?'

'Across the Powder River is Lakota territory and forbidden to buffalo hide hunters, Mr. Parker. I just wanted to get the location straight,' Caspar responded evenly. He had taken an instant dislike to Caleb Parker and, in a way, it worried him because he was not given to such reactions.

Caleb Parker became openly hostile. He growled, 'Now you've got the facts! So how's about quitting all this third degree and getting after my buffalo hides?'

'Mr. Ransome, you'll leave at sunup,' Major Collins ordered tersely. 'You'll take fourteen days rations and, you'll take Mr. Parker with you, so he can show you exactly where he killed his buffalo.' Caleb Parker's small eyes narrowed and his mouth tightened. 'Gentlemen, dismissed!' The officers present snapped to attention, saluted and left.

Captain Fetterman remained. He said, with a sardonic grin, 'I'll wager they don't get those hides back, Major.'

'And I'll wager fifty dollars that they do get them back, unless Mr. Shifty-eyed Caleb Parker killed those buffalo west of the Powder River.'

'You've got a bet, Major,' Captain Fetterman chuckled. 'Always did like to bet on a sure thing.'

CHAPTER TEN

Sunup of the fourth day found the patrol riding in the long shadow of Pumpkin Butte. Caspar and Lieutenant Ransome led the patrol, followed by Sergeant Hanna and Caleb Parker. Sergeant Hanna had taken care to ride on the upwind side of the hide hunter. He had also ignored all attempts at conversation by the man.

The patrol passed out of the shadow of Pumpkin Butte and Caspar started looking for familiar landmarks to get his bearings. After a while he said, 'George, we must be getting close to within six miles of the Powder River.'

Lieutenant Ransome turned in the saddle and called back, 'Mr. Parker, will you please join us?'

Caleb Parker kicked his mount and joined the two officers. Lieutenant Ransome said, 'Mr. Parker, Lieutenant Collins, who knows this country, tells me we're close to six miles from the Powder River, so we ought to be seeing signs of your kill pretty soon.'

'I'm keepin' my eyes peeled, Lieutenant,' Caleb Parker grunted. He dug a fresh cigar from his vest pocket and lit it.

The patrol dropped down a draw between two high bluffs which opened on a wide slope of plain, covered with the short buffalo grass. Presently, a wide depression appeared that was littered with the skulls and bones of buffalo.

'Thar it is!' Caleb Parker cried triumphantly. 'Thar's whar we made our first big kill! Satisfied now, Lieutenant?'

Lieutenant Ransome nodded, 'He's right. It occurred considerably this side of the Powder River, Caspar.'

'Maybe,' Caspar said. He rode forward, dismounted, and picked up some bones and examined them carefully. When he remounted, he carried two thigh bones with him and rejoined Lieutenant Ransome and Caleb Parker. He handed one of the bones to Lieutenant Ransome and explained, 'Bone is bleached and all dried out, George. The

100

buffalo must have been killed months ago.'

'You callin' me a liar, Lieutenant?' Caleb Parker demanded, belligerently.

'I don't have to!' Caspar retorted. He tossed the other bone to him. 'See for yourself.'

Caleb Parker went through the motions of examining the old bone, then tossed it disgustedly to the ground, pushed back his battered, weather-stained bowler hat, exposing the beginnings of the wide white streak in his thick red hair. His small, watery eyes scanned the terrain in assumed confusion, then he turned to discover both officers eyeing him askance.

'Well, maybe it were t'other side o' Pumpkin Butte we killed 'em!' he blustered. 'All those blasted buttes and valleys look alike to me, anyway.'

Caspar and Lieutenant Ransome exchanged meaningful looks. Caspar said, 'George, do you feel like indulging in a wild-goose chase?'

'Certainly not!'

'You mean you ain't agoin' to get me back my hides?' Caleb Parker flared up.

'If the Oglalas took them this side of the Powder River, you'll get them back, mister!' Caspar retorted cryptically.

'We're wasting time,' Lieutenant Ransome snapped. He raised his right arm, and gave a signal. 'Detail forward. Hi-yo!' The detail moved on and broke into a canter.

Caleb Parker dropped back to ride alongside Sergeant Hanna. He took the upwind side. Sergeant Hanna promptly changed places with him. 'Don't you ever take a bath, mister?' he asked.

'Thar's more important things than takin' a bath, soldier boy. Such as, when I get back to Bismarck, the complaint I'll lodge with the territorial governor thet them stinkin' Injuns are allowed to hunt anywhere, but the fuckin' Army says a white man's got to stop this side o' the Powder River!' Caleb Parker snarled.

Sergeant Hanna bristled. 'I'll stand for none of the likes of you running down the Army! So if you don't shut that big, ugly yap of yours, mister, I'll be happy to shut it for you!'

The afterglow of the setting sun sent red flames across the western sky from behind the distant Big Horn Mountains when the detail came to the Oglala camp, which was strung along the eastern bank of the Tongue River. At Caspar's suggestion, Lieutenant Ransome left the detail to make camp upstream outside the village while he, Caspar, Sergeant Hanna and Caleb Parker rode in. Dogs barked at the heels of their horses. A few of the young warriors and girls called friendly greetings to Caspar, who returned them in kind. This not only puzzled Caleb Parker, but caused his suspicions to rise.

In the great lodge of Spotted Tail, Evening

Star fed small sticks into the fire. She wore her deerskin breechcloth and beaded moccasins. Her golden body, still wet from her late afternoon swim in the river, glistened in the firelight. Her father squatted, smoking his pipe with Crazy Horse and Gray Wolf, his guest from the northern Cheyennes. Her mother sat further back from the men, sewing beads on a new pair of moccasins for Evening Star.

Hearing the sound of shod horses ride into the great lodge circle, Evening Star stepped quickly to the open flap and looked out. 'It is Cas!' she cried excitedly. 'He has two more Soldier Coats with him and an ugly white man, who looks like a buffalo hide hunter.'

Her father rose quickly and stepped out of his lodge, followed by Crazy Horse, Gray Wolf and Evening Star, just as Caspar, Lieutenant Ransome, Sergeant Hanna and Caleb Parker rode in and dismounted.

Lieutenant Ransome was instantly struck by the sheer beauty of Evening Star. His eyes dropped to her full, upright breasts. He said in an aside, 'You take care of Chief Spotted Tail, Caspar. I'll attend to the naked beauty.'

Caspar made no comment but raised his left hand, palm outward, in the peace sign. A quick hand motion from Chief Spotted Tail and some of the girls ran forward and took the horses away.

Caspar stepped to Chief Spotted Tail and,

with a slight bow, touched the tips of the fingers of his left hand to his forehead, as a mark of respect, and said, '*Woyuonihan.*'

Chief Spotted Tail's voice was faintly hostile, 'Cas comes with Soldier Coats at his back. Why is this?'

'The Soldier Coat Chief sent us to talk with Chief Spotted Tail about a small trouble between the Lakotas and some white hide hunters,' Caspar replied.

'Talk between friends is a good thing,' Chief Spotted Tail said. He motioned for Caspar and group to be seated.

As they squatted on the ground in a small circle, Caspar sat next to Chief Spotted Tail, then Lieutenant Ransome, Sergeant Hanna and Caleb Parker. Evening Star darted back into the lodge, to return with the ornate peace pipe and a flaming brand from the fire. She handed the pipe to her father and then held the flaming brand for him to light it. At the same time, she cast a covert glance at Caspar with eyes that were soft and warm. Caspar gave her a quick smile, then fastened his attention on Spotted Tail.

On the other hand, Lieutenant Ransome couldn't keep his eyes from Evening Star, her breasts in particular, and he found himself making an exception in her case to his inherent dislike for everything that was Indian.

Once the peace pipe was lighted, Evening

Star took her place, standing behind her father. Chief Spotted Tail puffed solemnly on the pipe, then handed it to Caspar.

Meanwhile, Caleb Parker had been squinting at Caspar, his anger rising at what he thought he saw. Behind one dirty hand he whispered to Sergeant Hanna, 'I know'd it! Know'd somethin' wuz wrong with Lieutenant Collins! He's got Injun in him. That's whut! Dadblamed right he has!'

'Try making something of it and I'll bash your face in,' Sergeant Hanna hissed back. Caleb Parker glared at him, but had the sense to keep quiet. He squinted again at Caspar.

Lieutenant Ransome took a few puffs on the pipe and handed it to Sergeant Hanna, only to return his interest to Evening Star. She became aware of his bold stare and anger flashed into her eyes, then they dropped to Caspar and they became warm again.

When Caleb Parker finished his turn at the peace pipe, Evening Star took it from him and returned it to her father's lodge.

'Now Cas will tell Spotted Tail about this small trouble between the Oglalas and the white hide hunters.'

Caspar pointed across the circle at Caleb Parker and said, 'That man claims that ten suns ago he and six other men killed forty buffalo and that the Oglalas took those buffalo from him. Are his words true?'

Spotted Tail closed his eyes in thought,

then he said, 'The words were true words. Crazy Horse did take those buffalo from this white hide hunter. Let him speak!'

Crazy Horse strode into the circle, cast an angry look at Caleb Parker, then with a slight bow, he touched the tips of the fingers of his left hand to his forehead to Chief Spotted Tail, and spoke. 'Hear me! The white hide hunters were hunting in the land of the Lakotas! We took their buffalo! We took their guns! Next time we will take their scalps!'

'He's a goddamn'd liar!' Caleb Parker exploded. Crazy Horse dropped a hand to the knife at his breech-cloth.

Caspar cut in strongly. 'Hear me, Crazy Horse! We have come to talk about this bad thing, not to fight!' Crazy Horse eased the grip on his knife but kept his angry gaze on Caleb Parker.

'Mr. Parker,' Caspar continued, 'one more such outburst from you and I shall suggest that Lieutenant Ransome order you out of camp!'

'Go ahead an' speak yore piece, Lieutenant,' Caleb Parker growled malevolently. He spat contemptuously in the dust.

Crazy Horse turned to Caspar and most of the hot anger washed from his eyes. He said quietly, 'Crazy Horse will listen to the words of his friend Cas.'

Caspar said, 'The white hide hunter says that he and his men killed the buffalo six miles beyond the Powder River. Can Crazy Horse prove that his words were not true words?'

'At sunup, Crazy Horse will lead the Soldier Coats toward the east, and when the sun is in the middle we will be only half the distance to the Powder River. There the Soldier Coats will find the new bones of the buffalo killed by these white hide hunters! They will find the ashes of their campfire! They will find the wheel marks of their wagons. They will find the tracks of their iron hoofed horses!'

Caspar turned to Caleb Parker. 'Do you still claim you were hunting six miles beyond the Powder, mister?'

'Standin' flatfooted on it! An' it's the Army's job to back me up!' Caleb Parker proclaimed.

'You're dead wrong, mister! The Army's job is to punish any man—white or red—who breaks the peace!' Caspar snapped. 'Lieutenant Ransome, I think Mr. Parker has contributed all he can to this talk. I suggest he be escorted back to camp!'

'Sergeant! Escort Mr. Parker back to camp!' Lieutenant Ransome ordered.

'On your feet, mister!' Sergeant Hanna said with satisfaction. He grasped Caleb Parker roughly by the arm and yanked him to his feet.

Caleb Parker, seething with anger, shouted at Caspar, 'Better make up yore mind which side yore on, you stinkin' half-breed!'

Sergeant Hanna's big fist landed a solid smash to Caleb Parker's jaw, knocking him out. Catching his body before it hit the ground, the sergeant slung it over his shoulder.

He grinned broadly as he snapped a salute to Lieutenant Ransome and said, 'I warned him, sir!' He stalked off with his burden, accompanied by the laughter, hoots and jeers of the delighted Lakotas. Chief Spotted Tail rose, followed by Caspar and Lieutenant Ransome.

Spotted Tail said, 'At sunup, Cas, Crazy Horse will prove that the words of the white hide hunter were bad words!' He turned and retreated to his lodge. Evening Star gave Caspar a lingering look and followed her father.

Lieutenant Ransome grimaced and shook his head. He said. 'While I think Caleb Parker is a goddamned liar, just the same Caspar, it set a damn bad precedent for the Army to manhandle a white man in front of the Lakotas. I'll have to put Sergeant Hanna on report.'

'You can add to that report, Mr. Ransome, that this was the first time that the Lakotas have learned they can expect any justice from the Army,' Caspar told him grimly.

'Oh, come on, Caspar, no need to get your feathers ruffled. You know I'm right,' Lieutenant Ransome rejoined lightly, in an attempt to smooth things over.

Crazy Horse joined them, with He Dog. He placed a hand on Caspar's shoulder. 'Cas has not forgotten his mother's people. It makes the heart of Crazy Horse feel good that this is so.'

'*Hohahe!*' He Dog chortled. 'The heart of that white hide hunter was bad toward everyone. He has no friends!' He tapped the scalping knife at his breech-cloth. 'He Dog would be happy to make his spirit walk away.'

Lieutenant Ransome's face reddened with anger. This was proof positive of what he had just told Caspar.

Caspar reproved He Dog sternly. 'If the white hide hunter has spoken with split tongue, the Soldier Coat Chief will punish him, not the Lakotas.'

Caspar saw Evening Star step out of her lodge opening. She paused, gave him a long look, turned away, glanced back at him over her shoulder, then made her way among the lodges, heading for the river.

Caspar returned to where the detail was camped with Lieutenant Ransome, the coolness between the two officers silently building. They found Caleb Parker sitting under the watchful eyes of Sergeant Hanna, his jaw noticeably swollen. He chewed on a dead cigar, saying nothing. His small eyes bored murderously at Caspar. Caspar said to Lieutenant Ransome, 'We can iron out our differences back at the fort. Meanwhile, I've got an appointment with Evening Star.'

Lieutenant Ransom replied, edgily, 'Dame Fortune didn't do too badly by me, but she just naturally slobbered all over you, at least as far as that beauty is concerned.'

'I thought you were the one who said he could find no beauty in an Indian, mister,' Caspar rejoined.

'There's an exception to every rule, mister,' Lieutenant Ransome smiled coldly. 'Evening Star is the exception.'

CHAPTER ELEVEN

Caspar came upon Evening Star as she emerged from the river from her swim. She had discarded her breech-cloth and moccasins, wearing only her virgin's rope, which every Lakota girl must wear until she is married. She smiled at Caspar and lay down among the ferns at the base of a cottonwood. Caspar dropped down beside her.

'Has Star been thinking about this love

thing?' he asked.

Her eyes searched his face tenderly. 'Yes, Cas, Star has given big thoughts to this love thing.'

Cas smiled. 'Close your eyes.' He leaned over and gently kissed her eyes. Then he found her lips. They were softly silken and cool from the river. He kissed them lightly at first, then more firmly and he felt them become warm and gradually part. At the same time his left hand caressed her full, right breast. He felt her breath quicken.

'That,' he said softly, 'is more of this love thing for Star to have big thoughts about.'

She was quiet for a moment, then said, 'My father has said that when the new moon hangs in the sky, Star may walk under the blanket with the one of her choice.'

'Who must be Cas,' he smiled. 'And to make sure Cas does have Star, tell him what presents he must bring her father.'

A small, worried frown appeared on her smooth forehead. She said, 'My father will ask for big presents, Cas. Ten red blankets, six ponies, a fast-shooting gun and one hundred bullets.'

Caspar kissed her and said, 'Cas will bring those presents for your father. Then he will take Star with him to the Soldier Fort where life in many ways will be different from the one she has known, but the differences will be good. There will also be things for Star to

111

learn. For instance, the word love is something often spoken between husband and wife. It will make the heart of Cas feel good to hear Star say "Star loves Cas! Star loves Cas!" Let the ears of Cas hear Star say that for the first time.'

'Star loves Cas,' she managed, and suddenly became very pleased with her accomplishment. His lips found hers again in a long, slow kiss. A kiss that he was delighted to discover was not at all one-sided.

Moments later he became aware of a long shadow that had fallen over them. He looked up to find that Crazy Horse stood beside them, his soft moccasins having made no sound among the ferns. He stood looking down at them, his face enigmatical, giving no sign of his inner emotions. He said quietly, 'The heart of Evening Star is no longer split between Crazy Horse and Cas.'

Caspar rose, helping Evening Star to her feet. There was sadness, yet resolution in her eyes when she said, 'The heart of Evening Star now belongs to Cas.' She bent down and donned her breechcloth and moccasins.

Caspar said, 'The strong bond of friendship between Crazy Horse, Cas and Evening Star must not be broken! It must remain as it was between Tashunka, Cas and Little Singing Stream, in the old days beside the Shell River.'

'And where the Soldier Coats came to kill

us. Soon they will come again!' Crazy Horse retorted.

Evening Star spoke up with spirit. 'Has Crazy Horse forgotten that today the Soldier Coats took the side of Crazy Horse against one of their own people?'

The anger in Crazy Horse's face eased and he smiled faintly as he placed a hand on Caspar's shoulder. 'All Soldier Coat Chiefs are not like my friend Cas. Throw away your soldier coat, Cas. Stay with your mother's people. We will hunt buffalo, Shoshones, Crows and Snakes together. And when the Soldier Coats come against us we will fight them too!'

Caspar shook his head. 'When Little Big Man asked Cas why he became Soldier Coat, Cas remembers Crazy Horse answering that Cas's father was a Soldier Coat Chief and that to follow in the moccasin tracks of his father was the honorable thing to do.'

Crazy Horse nodded and frowned. 'But suppose the grandfather in the Washington ordered Cas to ride against the Lakotas?'

This was a subject Caspar had long feared, one he had hoped to avoid. He said slowly, 'Cas would come. But he would come as a friend. He would talk with his mother's people and the trouble would blow away like the wind in the buffalo grass.'

'When the blood is hot, it is the talk that blows away,' Crazy Horse warned. 'And if that happened, Cas would not follow his heart, he would follow the orders of the grandfather in the Washington.'

He paced up and down a few moments, trying to reach a decision. Finally, he said, with obvious reluctance, 'As Cas knows, the father of Crazy Horse is Worm, the holy man, the dreamer of dreams. Many of his dreams come true. During the last moon, my father dreamed of a fight between the Lakotas and the Soldier Coats. When it was done, he saw Crazy Horse ride away carrying a dead warrior who wore the soldier's coat. The dead warrior was Cas.'

Evening Star cried out angrily, tearfully, 'Wakan Tanka would not permit such an evil thing! Evening Star sets her face against this bad talk!'

She ran to Caspar and buried her face against his tunic. He placed one comforting arm around her, his other hand he placed on the shoulder of his friend. He, seeking to placate her, said, 'Dreams are big things. But don't worry, Star, Crazy Horse and Cas will make sure that this dream does not come true.'

Shouts from among the trees broke the mood of the moment. Crazy Horse said, 'It is He Dog!' He cupped a hand to his mouth and hallooed, *'Hoye! Hoye!'*

He Dog came trotting through the trees, wearing his usual happy grin, closely followed

114

by Lieutenant Ransome.

'If He Dog followed the moccasin tracks of Evening Star, he knew he would find his friend Cas,' He Dog chuckled.

Lieutenant Ransome reluctantly moved his eyes from the full breasts of Evening Star and said, 'Didn't mean to intrude, Caspar, but I've got news for your friend Crazy Horse. Our trip tomorrow is off! Caleb Parker has cleared out!'

'He was afraid of what the new buffalo bones and the tracks of his wagons would tell,' Crazy Horse commented acidly.

'It's getting too dark to follow his tracks now. We'll go after him at sunup. I think sixty days in the guard house at Fort Laramie may teach Mr. Parker that the Army has more important things to do than go on his wild-goose chases!'

While he spoke, He Dog faded back among the trees.

Lieutenant Ransome's gaze was drawn back to Evening Star, but his question was for Caspar.

'Well, Caspar, aren't you going to introduce me to this barbaric nymph, or don't I rate socially?'

'Star, this is Lieutenant George Ransome,' Caspar did the honors. 'He is my friend.'

Lieutenant Ransome acknowledged the introduction with a casual salute and a leering grin.

115

Evening Star said evenly, 'The Soldier Coat with the eyes that eat me up! Star thinks he is not your friend, Cas!'

The lieutenant gave a forced laugh. 'Ho ho! A beaut, Caspar, but a troublemaker.'

She replied, 'A white buffalo robe is a holy thing. It gives the owner the power to see many things that are hidden.'

'You almost convince me,' Lieutenant Ransome smiled thinly.

Meanwhile, at the Lakota pony herd, He Dog, armed with war lance, bow and arrows, tightened the war rope on his pony, mounted and rode off into the twilight.

CHAPTER TWELVE

Sunup found the detail in mounted formation within the great lodge circle. Caspar and Lieutenant Ransome were dismounted, making a formal goodbye to Chief Spotted Tail, Evening Star and Crazy Horse. Many warriors, squaws, girls and young boys crowded the outer circle, their curiosity aroused by this close look at so many of the hated Soldier Coats.

Chief Spotted Tail, with his usual quiet dignity, said, 'This talk has been a big thing. The door of my lodge will always be open to my friend Cas.'

116

Caspar made a slight bow, touched the tips of the fingers of his left hand to his forehead. He turned to Evening Star and said softly, 'Cas will see Star before the new moon. Cas loves Star, remember?'

Her eyes became soft and warm and she repeated the words. Behind her Caspar could see Gray Wolf, the Cheyenne, glaring at him.

Caspar was exchanging the Lakota double handshake with Crazy Horse when He Dog rose into the great circle, howling gleefully and waving his war lance, from which dangled a fresh scalp, a familiar red-haired scalp that had a white streak running up the center. He knew that he was about to tangle with Lieutenant Ransome. He also knew that he would lose out, because Lieutenant Ransome outranked him.

The watching Lakotas howled their applause as He Dog pulled up and proudly flourished his gory trophy.

Addressing Caspar and Lieutenant Ransome he said gleefully, 'He Dog brings big present to his Soldier Coat friends! He has saved them heap of trouble!'

'Goddamn it, Caspar, that's Caleb Parker's scalp!' Lieutenant Ransome exploded.

He Dog's happy grin widened, '*Hohahe!* His spirit has walked away, leaving no friends to mourn him! Now Cas can ask the grandfather in the Washington to give He Dog a big present!'

117

Caspar said sternly, 'He Dog, the killing of a bad white man must be left to the Soldier Coats! The grandfather in the Washington, he will be very angry with He Dog for doing this bad thing!'

He Dog was outraged at Caspar's words. He pointed at Lieutenant Ransome and cried, 'Last night that Soldier Coat Chief said he wanted this bad one!'

Caspar tried to suppress a grin, but failed.

'He's right, George. You did say you would go after Parker at sunup. When a Lakota says he's going after a man, he means it is to kill him. And, so He Dog only thought he was doing you a favor.'

'I don't give a good goddamn what he thought,' Lieutenant Ransome snapped. 'The bastard's killed a white man! Sergeant Hanna!'

'Sir!' Sergeant Hanna gritted. He had never trusted Lieutenant Ransome. He didn't trust him now.

'Place this Indian under arrest!'

'First and second files, forward!' Sergeant Hanna ordered. He and two troopers spurred their mounts to block any escape by He Dog.

Howls of anger went up from the assembled Lakotas. Squaws and girls ran to bring weapons to the warriors not already armed.

'Cancel that order, George!' Caspar yelled. 'Or all hell will break loose!'

118

'Be damn'd if I will, mister!'

Crazy Horse spat angrily. 'If the Soldier Coats try to take He Dog to the Soldier Fort there will be a big fight.'

At that moment, death hung in the air. Sergeant Hanna's eyes were on Lieutenant Ransome, awaiting his next order, which he knew would be to draw sabers. Because it would be close fighting, in his mind he kissed the cross.

Caspar moved quickly to Chief Spotted Tail. He touched the tips of the fingers of his left hand to his forehead and said, 'Hear me! There has been a big misunderstanding! He Dog has killed a white man, a bad white man, but still a white man. Therefore, He Dog must go to the Soldier Fort, but he will not be taken there as a prisoner. He will go with us as a friend. There Cas will explain about this misunderstanding to the Soldier Coat Chief. He will tell him that He Dog thought he was being a big help to the Soldier Coats and the misunderstanding will walk away.'

'Taking a lot on your shoulders, aren't you, Mr. Collins?' Lieutenant Ransome rasped. 'Remember, I'm in command here!'

'I must remind you, mister, that Major Collins ordered you to leave all negotiations with the Lakotas to me!' Caspar retorted.

Lieutenant Ransome's mouth tightened, bridling his temper. 'Sergeant Hanna, have the guard return to ranks!'

'First two files, rejoin ranks!' Sergeant Hanna ordered, greatly relieved. The two troopers turned their mounts and rejoined the detail. Chief Spotted Tail gave Caspar a long look from his hooded eyes, then said, 'He Dog will go to the Soldier Coat Chief and Cas will explain about this misunderstanding.'

'Crazy Horse will ride there, also.' Crazy Horse cast an angry look at Lieutenant Ransome. 'To make sure that bad words are not spoken by another Soldier Coat Chief!'

'Evening Star will ride to the Soldier Fort also.' She darted into her lodge.

Caspar was instantly filled with apprehension. He had a vision of Evening Star riding barebreasted into Fort Laramie and of the commotion that would ensue; and more so, of the effect it would have on his father and particularly on Vic.

Caspar's worries were needless, for with He Dog and Crazy Horse as his riding companions—Lieutenant Ransome was no longer speaking to him—Evening Star soon caught up. She ranged her pinto alongside Caspar. She was beautifully dressed in a bleached deerskin smock, leggings, and moccasins, all highly decorated with beads and small porcupine quills.

'Star remembered about the love thing. Cas said that at the Soldier Fort a wife should not allow any Soldier Coat to see her breasts but her husband.'

Caspar smiled. 'Cas will be very proud to show Star to his father, the Soldier Coat Chief.'

For the first night camp was made on the east bank of the Powder River. Lieutenant Ransome elected to eat alone, having previously rejected any attempt by Caspar to talk reasonably about the situation. He had curtly stated that any talking he would do would be done at Headquarters.

Caspar ate his supper with Evening Star, Crazy Horse, He Dog, and Sergeant Hanna. As they ate, Caspar noticed that Evening Star was unusually quiet and withdrawn. Thinking that she was worried about what would happen to He Dog, he said, 'Don't worry about He Dog. The Soldier Coat Chief will not do anything to him.'

'Star is not worried about He Dog,' she replied quietly.

'Evening Star now talks like Soldier Coat,' He Dog teased.

'Star try to talk the way Cas has taught her!' she retorted indignantly.

'Lieutenant,' Sergeant Hanna said worriedly, 'I don't figger Lieutenant Ransome's worried about He Dog at all. I figger he's after your hide.'

'After my hide? How do you mean, Mike?'

'I saw the look in his eyes when you forced him to countermand his arrest order. It was a killing look, sir.'

121

'You're imagining things that weren't there, Mike. Lieutenant Ransome, right now, is all burned up, but he'll get over it by the time we reach Fort Laramie.'

'Wish I could agree with you, sir.'

When the last half of the old moon appeared above distant Pumpkin Butte, Caspar and Evening Star walked upstream to enjoy a swim in private. Evening Star was still disturbed and preoccupied. Caspar put an arm around her and said, 'Come on, now, Star, tell me what has been bothering you all evening.'

'First we swim. Then we make big talk.' She broke from him and ran ahead, seeking a secluded place to swim.

Evening Star came out of the water first. Caspar found her lying among deep ferns, staring up at the moonlit sky. As he sank down beside her, she surprised him by holding out her arms to him. She said, 'Star wants more of this love thing.'

His lips found hers in a gentle but prolonged kiss.

'Last night Star lay awake, thinking of this love thing. She went to the door of the lodge and looked out, and she saw the shadow of Yonke-lo pass by.'

'Well, there was almost a big killing in the great lodge circle today. Perhaps that was why the shadow of the god of death walked about, Star. But nothing happened,' Caspar

122

said.

Evening Star's apprehension was not lessened. She shook her head. 'Cas, when the shadow of Yonke-lo passed my lodge, it stopped, blotting out the moon, then it moved on. Yonke-lo was waiting for me, or, as Cas filled the pictures in my head, he was waiting for Cas. The bad dream of Worm, the holy man, the father of Crazy Horse, still walks behind me.'

'The dream where Crazy Horse rode away from a fight carrying the body of a Soldier Coat that Worm thought looked like me, forget it, Star. From now on all talks between the Lakotas and the Soldier Coats will be good talks.' Caspar sought to reassure her and he kissed her again. Her lips were warm, but gave him no response.

She placed his left hand on her right breast and moved closer to him. 'Evening Star is afraid for Cas, afraid that this love thing that will make us as one will fly away from us.'

Caspar took her in his arms and whispered, 'Pretty quick the new moon will come and Cas will give your father ten red blankets, six fine ponies, a fast-shooting rifle and a hundred bullets and Star will become the wife of Cas and live safely in the Soldier Fort, and this love thing will be very strong between us and we will become as one.'

Evening Star, still apprehensive, glanced over his shoulder, and among the dark trees she thought she saw a tall shadow moving, the shadow of Yonke-lo.

She caught her breath and a cold shiver passed through her body.

Caspar whispered, 'Star, what's the matter?'

Star made no reply, but her eyes searched his face tenderly, as though to imprint every facet of it permanently in her mind. Then she reached among her clothes in the ferns at her side and handed Caspar her hunting knife.

'Cas must cut the virgin rope of Star,' she said softly.

'Cas loves you, Star. He wants you! But to cut Star's virgin rope before she is married is against the law of the Lakotas.'

'This love thing that Star feels for Cas is bigger than the law of the Lakotas. She wants this love thing that will make us one. She wants it now, before any of these bad dreams become true dreams.'

Caspar no longer held back his own surging desire. He took the knife and carefully cut the narrow deerskin belt that supported her virgin's rope. Taking her in his arms, Caspar slowly, lovingly aroused the passion in her, an act no Lakota warrior had ever done for his woman. When he finally entered her, he did it gently at first. He felt her body tighten against the sudden pain, but there was no rejection on her part. Instead her shapely, long legs tightened about him, forcing a deeper penetration.

At last they lay quietly in each other's arms, fully and completely sated for the moment. Star whispered, 'Now this love thing is strong between Cas and Star and they are as one.'

Caspar kissed her gently. 'Yes, my darling, we are now as one, and all the bad dreams have now walked away.'

CHAPTER THIRTEEN

The flag hung listlessly from its pole outside Headquarters at Fort Laramie, not even a slight breeze stirred on that hot June morning. Tethered outside Headquarters were Evening Star's pinto, Crazy Horse's buckskin and He Dog's brown cayuse.

Out on the Parade, Corporal Big Mouth was trying to teach his platoon of Indian scouts the rudiments of the manual of arms with a marked lack of success. Two troopers wearing fatigues crossed from the stables, carrying buckets of water for the Lakota ponies. Sergeant Hanna paced the stoop. He was worried about what was taking place inside.

Caspar stood rigidly at attention, watching his father's face for possible reactions as the latter listened to Lieutenant Ransome's report. Captain Fetterman, his usual sardonic self, sat near the major, also listening. Crazy Horse and Evening Star sat on chairs to one side, their hostile gaze fastened on Lieutenant Ransome. He Dog squatted on the floor, his back to the wall, his eyes on the scalp of the late Caleb Parker on the major's desk as if it were the crown jewels.

'I am sure, sir,' Lieutenant Ransome said, stabbing a finger at the scalp, 'that you cannot fail to recognize that filthy red scalp with the white streak as having once belonged to the hide hunter, Caleb Parker!'

The major's face was expressionless. Caspar knew that his father was in a difficult situation. He also knew that he would lean over backwards to be strictly impartial in his judgement. The major said, 'At ease. Both of you, gentlemen.' He looked at He Dog. 'Why did He Dog kill that white hide hunter?'

He Dog pointed at Lieutenant Ransome and cackled, 'He said that the white hunter had ridden away, that at sunup he was going after him. It made He Dog's heart good to save his new Soldier Coat friends much trouble. Besides, it is a very fine scalp.'

Major Collins had difficulty maintaining a straight face. On the other hand, neither Captain Fetterman nor Lieutenant Ransome were amused.

'Mr. Ransome,' the major asked. 'Did you state, in the presence of He Dog, that at sunup you were going after Caleb Parker?'

Lieutenant Ransome's face reddened, 'Well, yes, sir, I did. I meant only to bring in Parker for punishment. I didn't mean to kill him!'

'Mr. Ransome,' the major explained quietly, 'For your information, when a Lakota goes after a man, he either kills him or is himself killed. Continue with your report, mister!'

Lieutenant Ransome's jaw set. He resented the rebuke, but he felt certain the major would change his tone quickly when he fired the rest of his ammunition.

'Sir, at sunup I had moved the detail into the great lodge circle for a formal goodbye to Chief Spotted Tail when He Dog rode in, brandishing Caleb Parker's scalp. He had obviously killed a white man and so I ordered Sergeant Hanna to place He Dog under arrest! However, Mr. Collins sided with the Lakotas against me. It was a case of flagrant insubordination, and, I believe, regulations call for a courtmartial, sir!'

Major Collins frowned. He gave Caspar a searching look and asked, 'Is this correct, Mr Collins?'

'Basically, yes, sir,' Caspar replied resolutely. 'But Lieutenant Ransome neglected to mention that Crazy Horse threatened to start a big fight if we persisted in the arrest of He Dog. My orders, sir, were to conduct all negotiations with Chief Spotted Tail and the Lakotas, not, I repeat, not, Lieutenant Ransome!'

Major Collins nodded. 'I gave you such orders! Mr. Ransome, did you hear Crazy Horse announce that he would fight?'

'Yes, sir, I did. But, in my opinion, Crazy Horse was merely showing off before his people. In other words, he was bluffing!'

'What is this bluffing thing?' Crazy Horse interrupted, suspiciously.

'Lieutenant Ransome meant that Crazy Horse would not use weapons to back up the big words from his mouth,' the major explained.

Crazy Horse retorted with quick anger. 'Had that one tried to take He Dog out of camp, only Cas would have returned to the Soldier Fort to tell how your Soldier Coats died.' He paused and his voice softened as he looked at Caspar. 'But Cas follows the Little Soldier Flag, and Crazy Horse thinks he would have raised weapons against the Lakotas. He would have died also, and the heart of Crazy Horse would have been in the ground.'

'Rashness of command is a quality an officer cannot afford, Mr. Ransome,' Major Collins said sternly. "Now, about He Dog. He misconstrued the meaning of what you said. Consequently, he thought that by killing Caleb Parker he was helping you.' He turned to He Dog. 'Hear me! If He Dog kills another white man, the Soldier Coats will arrest him and he will be punished. Does He Dog understand these words?'

He Dog bobbed his head and grinned. 'He Dog was happy to have helped his Soldier Coat friends.' His eyes returned to the fresh scalp on the major's desk.

The major took a deep breath and turned back to Lieutenant Ransome. 'Regarding your request that Mr. Collins face courtmartial proceedings. I would remind you, mister, that by interfering between Mr. Collins and the Lakotas, you disobeyed my direct orders! Further, that due to this rashness, or I shall be more than generous and say that due to your inexperience, you came close as hallelujah to costing the Army the lives of two junior officers and thirty-one enlisted men! Request that Mr. Collins face courtmartial proceedings denied! Mr. Ransome, you are dismissed!'

Lieutenant Ransome's face flamed with suppressed anger. His mouth tightened. He came up with a stiff salute, did a smart about-face and marched from the room.

The major turned to Captain Fetterman and remarked, 'I believe it has been established beyond the shadow of a doubt that Caleb Parker killed those buffalo west of the Powder, Captain.'

Captain Fetterman reached for his wallet

and said, 'And I owe you fifty dollars, courtesy of our beloved red brothers.'

Major Collins permitted himself a wry smile.

'Which the enlisted men's mess will, no doubt, appreciate.'

As Captain Fetterman began to count out his money, He Dog thought he had designs on his precious scalp. He leapt up, snatched it away and tucked it into the belt of his breechcloth.

'Damn it, Major,' Captain Fetterman cried, his anger at losing the bet doubling, 'You aren't going to allow him to keep that filthy thing?'

'That scalp means as much to He Dog,' Major Collins informed him, 'as our regimental colors do to us.'

He Dog, the practical joker, eyed Captain Fetterman's thick head of hair with the air of a connoisseur. He chortled, 'The Soldier Coat Chief has a very fine scalp.' His grin widened and he left the room with his swift, pigeon-toed gait.

Unconsciously, Captain Fetterman passed his hand over his thick, black hair.

Caspar said amiably, 'He Dog was only pulling your leg, Captain. He loves to make jokes, sir.'

'I wonder,' Captain Fetterman rejoined coldly, 'if Caleb Parker found his jokes equally amusing?'

Regan, the major's portly cook and personal orderly entered, came smartly to attention, and saluted.

'Yes, Regan?'

This was one of the few moments of importance Regan had experienced of late and, wanting to make the most of it, he smoothed his dragoon moustache before saying, 'Major, Mrs. Collins wants you to bring Lieutenant Collins, Evening Star and Crazy Horse home for dinner.'

Major Collins was startled and instantly glanced at his son. Both guessed the reason for the invitation.

'Mrs. Collins,' Regan continued, 'also invited Captain and Mrs. Fetterman, sir.'

Both Crazy Horse and Evening Star looked askance at Caspar. Captain Fetterman gave a short, barking laugh. 'Should prove a highly enlightening experience. Virginia and I will be delighted to accept, Major. With your permission, I'll go and tell Virginia. I'm sure she'll have some extra primping to do for this momentous occasion.' With a casual salute, he left the room. Evening Star gave Caspar another questioning look. Captain Fetterman's open antagonism toward Caspar and Crazy Horse, and herself, had not escaped her.

Major Collins said, 'Caspar, you don't have to accept Vic's invitation if you'd rather not.'

'Thanks for the out, Dad,' Caspar replied

evenly. 'But, to quote Captain Fetterman, this dinner of Vic's should prove to be a highly enlightening experience.'

Under the watchful eyes of Sergeant Hanna, He Dog busied himself tying his precious scalp onto the war rope of his pony. Green bottle flies buzzed around the gory trophy. Sergeant Hanna's nose wrinkled disdainfully. He Dog looked up from his labor of love and grinned. 'Green flies heap good. Eat up meat. Make less work for He Dog.

His attention was caught by the sound of Corporal Big Mouth's voice as he tried to march his platoon of Indian scouts past headquarters in some semblance of military decorum.

'*Hoye!*' he shouted. '*Hoye*, Big Mouth!'

Corporal Big Mouth, marching just ahead of his platoon, turned his head and saw He Dog. '*Hoye*, He Dog,' he shouted, somewhat condescendingly.

'Where did Big Mouth get the foolish Soldier Coat?' He Dog jeered.

Corporal Big Mouth came to a sudden stop. The first two files on his platoon piled into him. The following files bucked into one another. Corporal Big Mouth's anger flared up as he saw Major Collins, Caspar, Crazy Horse and Evening Star exit from Headquarters. He pointed viciously at the corporal's stripes on his sleeve and yelled back, 'Big Mouth now Little Soldier Chief!'

'*Hou! Hou!*' He Dog hooted derisively. 'Pretty quick He Dog chase Big Mouth all the way back to the grandfather in the Washington.'

'Sergeant Hanna, what the devil's going on?' Major Collins snapped and the sergeant came up with a smart salute.

'He Dog's only paying his respects to Corporal Big Mouth, sir!' he answered, tongue in cheek. Major Collins' mouth twitched. He said, 'Tell the mess sergeant I authorized a meal sent to He Dog, but first get busy and unscramble that God awful mess out there!'

'Yes, sir.' Sergeant Hanna saluted. He went down the steps fast, bellowing, 'Alright you stupid, grinning apes. Attenshun! Attenshun! Corporal Big Mouth, what the flaming, blazing hell—.'

CHAPTER FOURTEEN

Victoria had been sitting on the veranda, knitting a pair of socks that were to be a birthday present for Caspar. She saw the detail return, together with three Indians, and as soon as the detail dismissed, she had sent Regan to find out what was happening from the troopers. She didn't dare send him to

Headquarters. Being an officer's daughter, she knew that such procedure was strictly against regulations. But, being a woman, she was very inquisitive, because, even at that distance, she could see that one of the Indians was a girl.

When Regan returned with the information that the Indian girl was Evening Star, Victoria's growing apprehension rose sharply. Her fear that Caspar was headed hell-for-leather to at least stifle, if not ruin, his army career became very real. Determined to do what she could to prevent this, what to her mind would be a disaster, she had sent Regan with the message to her husband, Rufus, to bring Caspar, Evening Star and Crazy Horse to her home for dinner, in the hope that the marked contrast between the Lakota and an army officer's way of life would make him see the utter impossibility of such a marriage.

To help this contrast to be fully exploited, she had also invited Captain and Virginia Fetterman. Victoria was not particularly fond of the latter, who came from a prominent Baltimore family and was something of a snob, but knew she could be counted upon to render a yeoman's service in making Caspar realize the impossibility of such a union.

When Captain and Virginia Fetterman arrived, the former said, as Victoria seated them in the parlor, 'I've already briefed

Virginia on who, or should I say, on whom is coming to dinner, Vic.'

'One must admit one has to admire your courage, Victoria,' Virginia remarked loftily.

Captain Fetterman snorted, 'Oh, for heaven's sake cut out the Baltimore bushwah, Virginia, and prepare to witness the greatest Western comedy in history. Right, Vic?'

Victoria brushed a hand to her hair to mask her annoyance. Her motives were purely to help Caspar. There was no malice in her makeup.

She sighed and sank into a chair, saying, 'William, I don't think it will turn out to be a comedy, but it might well become a tragedy. Anyway, thank goodness Regan has dinner about ready to serve; and I imagine Caspar's friends would rather eat than talk. Frankly, I'd be at a loss to know what to talk to them about.'

'Oh, the usual, Vic,' Captain Fetterman laughed lightly. 'How to avoid taking a bath, the finer techniques of removing scalps— things like that.'

'Imagine,' Virginia laughed, 'having dinner with savages. I only hope they are housebroken.'

Victoria said, in quiet admonition, 'Rufus tells me that the Oglalas are an extremely courteous people and quite well-mannered.'

'If anyone ought to know, it's the major,' Captain Fetterman remarked sardonically.

Victoria did not miss his double entendre. 'But I fancy that Caleb Parker might not agree.'

As they arrived at his father's quarters, Caspar glanced down at Evening Star and noticed that she seemed excited and nervous. He took her arm and patted her hand. 'Star will like my father's wife. She is a very wonderful person.'

'Star will like the wife of Cas' father,' she assured him.

Major Collins said, giving Caspar a meaningful look, 'You three go in first, Caspar. I'll form a rear guard.'

Victoria rose as Caspar came in. He was between Crazy Horse and Evening Star and held each by the arm. Victoria's eyes widened as she saw Evening Star's compelling beauty. Captain Fetterman lifted an interested eyebrow at Evening Star, then glanced to see if his wife had noticed his reaction. She had.

Caspar said, 'Vic, may I present two friends of mine of long standing. Evening Star, I call her Star for short, and Crazy Horse.' Evening Star and Crazy Horse bowed their heads lightly and touched their foreheads with the tips of the fingers of their left hands.

Victoria smiled and said graciously, 'I am the new wife of Major Collins, the father of Caspar. Captain Fetterman you have already met. This lady is the wife of Captain

Fetterman.' Crazy Horse and Evening Star gravely touched their foreheads to Virginia Fetterman, who managed a forced smile in return.

Caspar placed his arm around Evening Star and said, 'Lovely, isn't she, Vic?'

Vic saw the good-natured challenge in his eyes. She replied, a little breathlessly, 'Yes, Yes, I'm afraid she is, my dear. Rufus, Regan has dinner ready to serve and I'm sure we are all hungry, so why don't we adjourn to the dining room?'

'Caspar, suppose you escort our guests in,' Major Collins said.

As they entered the dining room, Major Collins moved close to Victoria and whispered, 'Vic, what the devil are you up to?'

Her chin lifted resolutely. She whispered back, 'The answer to that is close to both our hearts, Rufus.'

Regan stood stiffly beside the door to the kitchen, immaculate in his white jacket and dragoon moustache, waxed and shining. The dining table glistened with a white lace banquet cloth, silver and crystal. Caspar's mouth tightened when he saw to what lengths Victoria had gone to embarrass Evening Star and Crazy Horse, who had never used anything but their fingers or a buffalo horn spoon to eat with. He eyed Victoria resentfully as he seated her at the far end of the table, near the kitchen door. She returned his look with a small, but sad little smile.

Caspar said, 'Crazy Horse will sit there.' He indicated the chair to Victoria's right. 'Star will sit here,' he indicated and pulled back the chair to Victoria's left and seated her.

Victoria said, 'Aren't you making a mistake, Caspar? Star is the main guest. She should be seated on my right.'

With assumed innocence, Caspar said, 'Why, Vic, I'm surprised at you. Don't you know that among the Lakotas it is the warrior who is the important guest. His squaw stands behind him while he eats. She eats later. Sorry, Vic, but squaws don't rate socially. With, of course, the exception of Star. She's the daughter of a Chief, so she will sit here, right next to me.'

Meanwhile, Major Collins had seated Virginia Fetterman on his right and her husband on his left. Caspar picked up the folded, snowy-white napkin in front of Evening Star, shook it out and spread it on her lap. 'This is some of the white man's foolishness. Star will use it to wipe her fingers and her mouth when she is finished eating.'

Evening Star gave him a questioning smile, having sensed the tension between him and Victoria. Crazy Horse, somewhat puzzled, followed suit with his own napkin.

Victoria said, 'Regan, you may start
138

serving.'

'Right away, ma'am.' Regan moved quickly into the kitchen.

An ominous silence pervaded the dining room. Crazy Horse was obviously ill at ease. Evening Star was also, until she felt Caspar's hand on hers. Major Collins cleared his throat. He said, 'My compliments on your table, Vic. All the silver, crystal, your grandmother's favorite lace banquet cloth—you've really put on the dog.'

'This is a very special occasion, Rufus,' she countered, aware he felt she had gone too far.

Regan reappeared and began placing large plates piled with roast beef, vegetables and gravy before the guests.

Virginia took a deep breath and managed a gracious smile. 'We do not stand on ceremony here,' she said, selecting a knife and fork from the glittering array beside her plate. She began cutting into her roast beef.

Evening Star and Crazy Horse watched Victoria using her knife and fork with apprehension.

Caspar deliberately broke up Victoria's carefully laid plans. Spurning the use of knife and fork, he picked up a dripping slice of roast beef with his fingers and tore into it Lakota style. Evening Star and Crazy Horse instantly followed suit.

Victoria turned pale. She glanced down the table at her husband and, to her dismay, saw that he was also eating with his fingers. Captain Fetterman shrugged and did likewise.

'Sorry, but I'm not that primitive,' Virginia snapped as she jabbed her fork viciously into her roast beef.

'Why, ladies, some of the tastiest meals I ever had were eaten without benefit of knives and forks,' the major commented with slight malice.

Slowly Victoria put down her knife and fork and commenced using her fingers.

Caspar, eating with gusto, nodded at Crazy Horse and said, 'Texas steer.'

Crazy Horse, his mouth full, grinned, 'Good, but not as good as buffalo hump!'

'Speaking of buffalo,' Captain Fetterman entered the conversation silkily, addressing Evening Star. 'Is it true that the squaws drink the blood of a freshly killed buffalo while it is still warm?'

Evening Star paused in her eating. Her wide, dark eyes rested calmly on this man she knew to be an enemy.

She said, 'The warm blood of the buffalo makes the hearts of the squaws hot toward their husbands.'

Captain Fetterman's eyes narrowed. He realized he was getting back better than he gave.

'The pale woman,' Evening Star continued, 'should drink often of the warm buffalo

140

blood. She would then bring big pleasure to her husband.' She regarded Virginia Fetterman gravely, but there was faint laughter in her dark eyes.

Virginia Fetterman was speechless. Nothing so outrageous had ever been said to her in Baltimore.

Her husband gave his short, barking laugh and said, 'By George, Virginia, she's got a point there!'

'Really, William,' his wife fired back, 'one doesn't mention such vulgarities. Especially not at the dinner table.'

Major Collins flushed angrily. He was on the point of demanding that the Fettermans apologize to Evening Star when Caspar spoke. He, too, was angry, but he kept that anger out of his voice. 'Vic, Dad, Captain and Mrs. Fetterman, before these not so oblique innuendos get out of hand, there is something I have to tell you. Vic, within three weeks you'll have another occasion to break out the silver and crystal and to use your grandmother's favorite lace banquet cloth. Because I'll be bringing Star back again to Fort Laramie. And this time, she will be my wife.'

Victoria's hand flew to her throat. 'Your wife? Caspar, but what about Crazy Horse? I thought he also wanted her?'

Crazy Horse said quietly, 'Crazy Horse wants Evening Star for his wife. But Crazy

Horse would not allow the shadow of a woman to come between Crazy Horse and his friend Cas.'

Victoria shot an agonizing glance at her husband.

'Aren't you rather rushing things, Caspar?' his father asked.

'Dad,' Caspar replied, 'Chief Spotted Tail has told Star that at the coming of the new moon she may choose a husband.' His hand dropped affectionately over Star's. 'The husband she will choose will be me.'

Star lifted her head proudly. 'Star will be happy to walk under the blanket with Cas.' She turned to Victoria and continued, 'Cas has taught Star the meaning of this love thing. It has become a big and strong thing between us. It has made Star and Cas as one!'

Major Collins pushed back his chair, rose and stopped behind Star's chair. He placed his hands gently on her shoulders. 'Vic,' he said, 'it seems we are about to add another beauty to the Collins family.' He bent down and kissed Star on the forehead.

Sergeant Hanna stood on the veranda of Headquarters, watching He Dog squatting on the ground beside his pony, wolfing down his dinner. Army scout Jim Bridger came through the fort gates and curved across the Parade to pull his lathered mount up sharply before Headquarters. He held his reins in his left hand and a bottle in his right. He swayed in the saddle, obviously drunk.

'The major inside?' He hiccoughed at Sergeant Hanna, as he fought his rearing horse.

'No, Jim, he's down at his own quarters.'

Jim Bridger clapped spurs to his mount and galloped off in the direction of Officer's Row.

'Hey! You can't see the major now, you blasted, drunken old goat!' Sergeant Hanna yelled and took off after Jim Bridger on the dead run.

In the dining-room, Captain Fetterman had arranged his face into a facade of affability. He was talking to Crazy Horse. 'And for the life of me I can't understand why the Lakotas choose to live in the wilds, sometimes hungry, often cold, when they could live on a reservation and have plenty of good food and warm blankets.'

Crazy Horse's soft reply was tinged with hostility. 'The Soldier Coat Chief forgets that this is the land of the Lakotas! The land of Pa Sapa, the sacred Black Hills! It is the Lakotas who should say to the whites, "Here you must live, but only here!"'

'You've got to admit Crazy Horse has a good point there, sir. After all, this is the land of the Lakotas,' Caspar remarked.

'Rather strange words coming from an officer of the Third, don't you think, Major?' Captain Fetterman commented acidly.

'Strange words, Captain, that happen to be true. Twenty-five years ago when I was first posted to the Indian frontier, Fort Laramie was not a military establishment. It was a white fur-trading post and this was the land of the Lakotas. Then the land grabbers put pressure on the Bureau of Indian Affairs, and their agents began giving presents to the Indians, blankets, tobacco, molasses, etc. Later, the presents were exchanged for Indian land.

'When too much land was grabbed and the Indians rebelled,' he continued, 'the Army was sent into the area to protect the agents and the land grabbers. Later, an uneasy peace prevailed and is still in effect. But—' The major broke off his talk as Jim Bridger burst into the room, to stand drunkenly, spraddle-legged, staring red-eyed at him.

'Major! All hell's busted out!' he hiccoughed loudly.

'Major, this man ought to be tossed in the guard-house. He's drunk as a skunk!'

'So'd you be, Cap'n if yore wife's belly'd been saber slit, an' the little 'un inside pried out!' Jim Bridger shot back.

CHAPTER FIFTEEN

Victoria and Virginia gasped in shock. Caspar rose quickly, took Jim Bridger by the arm, and pulled up a chair for him. 'Better sit down, Jim,' he said.

Sergeant Hanna burst in, snapped to a salute. He was red in the face and sweating from his run.

'Sorry, Major, but he got away from me. Come along, Jim.'

'At ease, Sergeant,' Major Collins said. 'I believe Jim has something important to tell us. Now, Jim, you know that Yellow Moon, your wife, is safe in Black Kettle's Northern Cheyenne village on Sand Creek where the Indian agent told them to camp.'

'She wuz safe, Major, until dawn three days ago when Colonel Chivington an' nine hundred of his bloody Colorado Volunteers jumped the village, slaughtered some two hundred and eighty men, women an' kids. Among the women killed were Black Kettle's wife an' my Yaller Moon.'

'Jim, are you absolutely sure this happened,' Caspar asked gently.

'Sartain sure, Lieutenant!' He took a swig from his bottle, then continued. 'I come upon Dull Knife and a small war party o' Northern Cheyennes. They'd catched up with five o'

145

them bloody Colorado Volunteers and chopped 'em up. Chopped 'em on account o' whut they found in their pockets.'

'What was that, Jim?' Caspar asked.

Jim Bridger wiped his eyes on a greasy, buckskin sleeve. 'They found scalps, Lieutenant, women's scalps. Not the kind taken from the top o' the head. These were cut from the crotch!'

Virginia gasped and seemed about to faint. Victoria was instantly at her side. 'Rufus, I—I'll take Virginia to the bedroom. I think we'd both better lie down awhile.'

'Yes, yes, by all means, Vic,' the major said.

Jim Bridger focused his eyes on Crazy Horse, whose face was already dark with anger. 'Black Kettle had guards out watchin' the pony herd, Crazy Horse. Know how all them nine hundred Colorado Volunteers sneaked past without the guards seein' 'em? They wuz guided down a narrow gully where the guards couldn't see 'em and sound the alarm. They wuz guided by a Lakota name of Little Big Man.'

'So Little Big Man got another Soldier Coat,' Caspar rasped bitterly.

'An' somethin else,' Jim Bridger added, 'Dull Knife told me Black Kettle wuz fixin' to lead what's left o' his people northwest, to carry the war pipe to the Lakotas!'

Crazy Horse shot a challenging look at

146

Caspar. Caspar could see the pent-up fury he was holding in check. Crazy Horse said, 'If the words of Big Throat are true words, Chief Spotted Tail will smoke the war pipe with Chief Black Kettle and the Lakotas will join their Northern Cheyenne cousins to fight the Soldier Coats!'

'Better toss this hothead in the guardhouse, Major!' Captain Fetterman snapped. 'Be one less of those red hellions to fight!'

Crazy Horse jumped to his feet. One hand dropped to the knife at his deerskin belt.

'You are out of order, Captain!' Major Collins said sharply. 'Crazy Horse is a guest!' He turned to Crazy Horse. 'The Soldier Coats who did this evil thing were not true Soldier Coats. Most of the time they work in the mines and saloons around Denver. Only sometimes they put on Soldier Coats! But they will be rounded up and be severely punished. Caspar, you will escort our guests safely off the post!'

As Caspar helped Evening Star from her chair, he said earnestly, 'Star does not have to leave. She can stay here and marry Cas.'

Her eyes filled. She shook her head slowly and said, 'There will be many who are wounded and sick, and Star will need to take care of these helpless ones.'

She turned away sadly, touched the tips of the fingers of her left hand to her forehead to Major Collins and left the room, followed by

Caspar. Crazy Horse paused before the major and said quietly, his hot anger eased momentarily, 'Crazy Horse thinks that the Soldier Coat Chief still carries the picture of Pretty Valley in his heart.' He touched the tips of his fingers of his left hand to his forehead and left the room.

Major Collins smashed his right fist into the palm of his left hand viciously and exploded angrily, 'What the god-damned hell made that bastard Chivington pull an insane massacre like that?'

'I kin answer that, Major,' Jim Bridger hiccoughed. 'That Chivington's got a stranglehold on the politics an' most o' the saloons and dancehalls in Denver. An' its his Colorado Volunteers that's his bully boys thet makes sartain sure he keeps thet stranglehold.'

The major nodded. 'I've heard several rumors to that effect,' he said cryptically.

'Then maybe yo' heard, too, thet Washington's about to induct them Colorado Volunteers into the Regular Army. An' next month they ship back East to join the Army of the Potomac.'

'What?' The major erupted. 'Are you saying that Colonel Chivington deliberately massacred those Cheyennes to provoke an Indian war so that the Colorado Volunteers would have to remain here on the frontier?'

Jim Bridger took another swig from his

bottle, nodded and said, 'Thet stranglehold Chivington's got on Denver pays off real big, Major. He don't figger to lose it.'

An orderly entered, saluted smartly and handed the major a telegram. The major scanned it quickly and the lines in his face deepened. He announced gravely, 'Headquarters has confirmed the Sand Creek Massacre! Colonel Chivington is at Fort Lyon under arrest awaiting courtmartial!'

'Army's spread out pretty thin all along the frontier, Major,' Captain Fetterman commented thoughtfully. 'But it ought to be able to handle the Northern Cheyennes and Oglala-Lakotas.'

'Who'll be joined by the Minneconjous, the Hunkpapas, the Sans Arcs, the Brules, the Bad Faces, the No-Bows—which means the whole Sioux Nation,' Jim Bridger put in acidly.

'Plus the Southern Cheyennes, the Kiowas an' the Arapahoes. Take some handlin' Cap'n.'

The hot noonday sun blazed down on the sloping hills, turning the short buffalo grass yellow and brown. Caspar, Evening Star, Crazy Horse and He Dog drew rein where the trail topped a ridge. Looking back they could see, through the noonday haze, the walls and watchtowers of Fort Laramie and catch the glint of the Platte River where it curved below the fort.

149

The three Lakotas turned their mounts to face Caspar, their dark eyes searched his face for some clue to his inner thoughts. The silence was broken only by the horses, shaking their heads and snorting to rid themselves of the flies that sought the soft moisture of their eyes and nostrils.

The unspoken question in the minds of his friends came through loud and clear to Caspar. He knew they wanted him to come with them. More than that, after that brutal depredation committed by white men wearing soldier uniforms, they expected him to heed the call of his blood and side with his mother's people.

Finally, when the silence became too oppressive, he said, 'Crazy Horse will tell Chief Spotted Tail that when the Soldier Coat Chief understood why He Dog killed the white hide hunter, he did not punish He Dog. That was a good thing! Crazy Horse must also tell Chief Spotted Tail that fighting and killing can only bring big sorrow to the lodges of the Lakotas. Tell Chief Spotted Tail that the Soldier Coats will not come against the Lakotas with weapons unless the Lakotas strike first!'

Crazy Horse's reply was decisive and faintly hostile. 'Hear me, Cas! If Chief Black Kettle carries the war pipe to Chief Spotted Tail, the Lakotas will fight! They will attack all whites they can find!' His voice softened.

'Evening Star has words to say to Cas!'

He turned his buckskin and rode on with He Dog. Evening Star heeled her pinto pony close to Caspar.

She said, 'At the Soldier Fort, Cas has enemies—the one called Fetterman and the one called Ransome. It is a bad thing to live among enemies. Among the lodges of the Lakotas Cas has no enemies. Cas will also have Star and this love thing that is so big and strong between them.'

Her nearness sent a surging through his blood, a wild longing to be with her. For a moment he felt the impulse to resign his commission and revert to his Indian heritage. Then, coming faintly from the fort, he heard the trumpet notes of a fatigue call, and he stiffened in the saddle, drawing himself back into his other half-world, the world of his father, of West Point, of the United States Army.

'Hear me,' he said gently. 'Cas cannot go with Star. He must remain here and follow the orders of his Soldier Chief. When the trouble has walked away, Cas will find the lodge of Chief Spotted Tail, and when he does will he find Star waiting?'

'This love thing that is between us is big and strong. Wana Tanka will not let it be broken.' Her eyes became misty as she spread both hands over her heart, then gradually opened them, like a flower responding to the

151

first rays of the morning sun. Star had given Caspar her heart in the old Lakota way. She turned her pinto pony and rode away after Crazy Horse and He Dog.

For several minutes Caspar stared after Evening Star and her companions until they dropped into a dip in the trail and vanished. His hands tightened on the cantle of his saddle, until the knuckles showed bone white. He had a gnawing fear in the pit of his stomach that he should never have let her go, that he should have found some way of persuading her to remain at the fort, that something might happen to her in the fighting. Already the bodies of many dead squaws and girls of the Northern Cheyennes lay dead at Sand Creek. The only place she would be safe would be at Fort Laramie.

Preoccupied with his worries about Evening Star, Caspar did not hear the approaching rider until he was almost upon him. It was Sergeant Hanna. His first reception to his old friend was not friendly. He said edgily, 'Afraid I might not be coming back, Mike?'

'Nothing could be further from my mind, Lieutenant,' Mike replied, innocently, as he dismounted and felt the left front fetlock of his big gray. 'Fact is, on the last patrol, Hank here stepped in a prairie dog hole and came up lame. Been rubbing it with liniment. Was just exercising him to see if he'd bowed a

152

tendon.' As if to show Sergeant Hanna he was feeling fine, Hank danced as his master remounted.

'No bowed tendon, and, I think, no prairie dog hole either. You're a poor liar, Mike.' Mike grinned.

Sergeant Hanna pushed his hat back and scratched his head. He said, 'Well, Lieutenant, now that you mention it, I was a mite worried on account of Evening Star's so downright beautiful. If it was me she was interested in I'd be sore tempted to desert heaven itself to be with her.'

'For your private information, Mike,' Caspar nodded, 'I almost did go with her. I'm worried about her. If general fighting should break out, army tactics call for hitting the villages when possible. That always means some women and kids are bound to get hurt.'

'Hell of a situation,' Sergeant Hanna agreed. 'Anyway, they've got that bastard Colonel Chivington under arrest at Fort Lyon. He's up for a courtmartial. Word came over the telegraph just before I left.'

'They should turn Chivington over to the Northern Cheyennes!'

'And the first thing they'd do would be to cut off his left arm.'

'You're wrong there, Mike. That'd be the last thing they'd cut off!'

'A thought, Lieutenant,' Mike grinned wickedly. 'A lovely thought.'

'We'll take it easy going back to the fort, Mike. I wouldn't want old Hank to bow a tendon.'

'The Lieutenant is most considerate,' Mike returned gravely.

He touched spurs to Hank's flanks and headed back for the fort at a dead run. Caspar let go a Lakota war whoop and sent his big appaloosa thundering after him.

CHAPTER SIXTEEN

Victoria wandered aimlessly about her living room, straightening a picture here, moving a piece of bricabrac there. She knew that both Rufus and Caspar were angry with her, and she was not too pleased with herself either. Virginia Fetterman sat, pretending to read a copy of the *Saturday Evening Post*, watching her friend. She said with a shrug, 'Really, Vic, I can't for the life of me see why you're so upset. After all, it was only a dinner party that went, well, sort of blew up.' She laughed. 'But, just think what a marvelous conversation piece it will make for years to come.'

Victoria turned. She said sharply, 'Apart from what Jim Bridger had to tell, I don't expect anything that happened at dinner to be repeated!'

154

Virginia made a small, amused reply, 'Alright, alright! So it'll be a closed subject, Vic.'

Victoria moved to the window, and stood looking out across the sunbaked Parade. 'I—I'm not very proud of what I did, Virginia. It was small and mean of me to do that to Caspar.'

'Oh, come on now, Vic. You put on a great show and Caspar's young. He'll survive. After all, she was only an Indian girl.'

'Only an Indian girl,' Victoria repeated slowly. 'And the most beautiful girl I've ever seen. I can't blame Caspar for falling in love with her.'

'As my husband, who admits he knows everything, says, and I quote, "One doesn't lower oneself to marry an Indian girl anymore." Unquote.'

Through the window, Victoria had seen Caspar and Sergeant Hanna ride in and dismount. A striker took their horses. Sergeant Hanna headed for the sutler's store. Caspar was coming down Officers' Row to go to his own bachelor quarters.

'Excuse me, Virginia,' she said hurriedly.

She was standing at the little picket gate in front of her home when Caspar came along. He stopped, touched his campaign hat politely, but with reserve. Victoria realized he was not going to make what she had to say any easier.

155

She said, 'Caspar, I—I'm sorry.'

'We must all do what we think is right,' he returned woodenly.

'Thank you, Caspar. That was more than generous of you.'

A trumpet call sounded urgently through the heat.

'Officers' call,' Caspar snapped. 'I've got to go, Vic!' He turned back toward Headquarters.

'Caspar,' Vic called. He paused and looked back.

'There was only one real lady at dinner today. Her name was Evening Star. I think she will make you a wonderful wife.'

Caspar ran back, kissed her on the cheek and hurried toward Headquarters, joining several other officers moving swiftly in the same direction.

When the officers had assembled, Major Collins said, 'At ease, gentlemen. Find chairs if you can. You've all heard about the massacre at Sand Creek of Black Kettle's Northern Cheyennes by the Colorado Volunteers, commanded by Colonel Chivington, who is presently under arrest at Fort Lyon.'

He paused to light a cigar. There were low mutterings of anger among some of the officers present. Mutterings that Captain Fetterman did not share in. He maintained his usual sardonic half smile as he blew a

156

smoke ring from his cigar. Slaughtering of the Indians bothered him not in the least.

'Jim Bridger reported that the remaining Northern Cheyennes, led by Black Kettle, Dull Knife and Little Wolf, were carrying the war pipe to Chief Spotted Tail of the Oglala-Lakotas,' Major Collins continued. 'I'd have liked to have had Jim Bridger here, but he is, I'm told, at present sleeping off a monumental drunk.' His voice dropped. 'Jim's Cheyenne wife was mutilated and killed in the massacre.'

He turned to Caspar. 'Mr. Collins, when you escorted Crazy Horse, He Dog and Evening Star off the post, was anything said about what Chief Spotted Tail's reaction would be when he receives the war pipe?'

'Yes, sir,' Caspar replied. 'Crazy Horse told me that, because the Cheyennes were their cousins, once the Oglalas receive the war pipe they would be obligated to hit the war trail. That would mean the Hunkpapas, too, and the Brules, the Sans Arcs, the No Bows, the Bad Faces and the Minneconjous, which means the whole Lakota nation, or the Sioux Nation as we call them. Crazy Horse said practically the same thing at dinner, sir.'

'And, it seems that General Headquarters in Omaha is of the same opinion. I am in receipt of telegraphic orders to prevent Black Kettle's Northern Cheyennes from reaching the Lakotas at all costs. Peaceably if possible,

157

if not by force!'

'That means we'll have to use force, Major. Force is the only thing those red devils understand!' Captain Fetterman said.

'I am hopeful of stopping Black Kettle peacefully, Captain,' Major Collins said crisply.

Captain Fetterman caught the major's tone of reproof, but it did not deter him. He touched a match to his cigar and asked smugly. 'You have a prescription for accomplishing this miracle, of course, sir?'

'Better a miracle than a firebrand, Captain,' the major remarked cryptically. He rose, stepped to a large topographical wall map of the area. 'Here's Sand Creek, and here is where Chief Spotted Tail has his camp on the Tongue River. The massacre occurred five days ago, which means the Northern Cheyennes have been moving northwest for that period of time. However, their rate of progress will have been slowed considerably by their sick and wounded on travois. I doubt if they have made more than fifteen miles a day. He turned to Caspar. 'Mr. Collins!'

'Sir!'

'In your considered opinion, would Black Kettle remain with his necessarily slow traveling people, or would he ride ahead to carry the war pipe to Spotted Tail?'

Without any hesitation, Caspar said, 'The Cheyennes are like the Lakotas, sir, they place the safety of their children, sick, wounded, women and girls ahead of everything else. Black Kettle would make the slow trek with his people to protect them from possible further outrages from the militia.'

'Another question, mister! Where would you say Black Kettle will have his people cross the North Platte River?'

'Spring was late this year, sir, so was the snow runoff. The North Platte is still in flood. The safest place for Black Kettle's people to ford it with all their travois would be at the shallows at the Platte River Crossing.

Major Collins nodded and pointed to a spot on the map. 'As most of you gentlemen know, the Platte River Crossing is here.' He resumed his seat behind his desk. 'Within the hour, I'm dispatching six transport wagons loaded with blankets, food and medical supplies. Contract Surgeon Lunt will go along to attend the sick and wounded Cheyennes. Troops A and B will serve both to escort and to put up a show of force, force that is to be used only as a last resort. Captain Fetterman will command! Any questions?'

Captain Fetterman snubbed out his cigar and said, 'I would remind the major that two troops of cavalry amount to about one hundred and fifty officers and enlisted men. Not a very impressive show of force. I respectfully request permission to take along a battery of howitzers. Only for a show of force, Major. But many of the Indians know that a howitzer shell can create one hell of a lot of havoc! That's the kind of force they respect, Major!'

Major Collins frowned, considered a moment, then said, 'Permission granted, Captain.' He turned again to Caspar. 'Mr. Collins!'

'Sir!'

'It's roughly one hundred and ten miles to the Platte River Crossing from here. How soon can you get there?'

Caspar thought briefly, then said, 'I can make it in about seven hours, if I take along a spare mount, sir.'

'Good,' Major Collins said. 'I'll detail Sergeant Hanna to accompany you. You'll leave at once, and if you should encounter the Northern Cheyennes before the column arrives, try to get across to Black Kettle that food, blankets and medical supplies are on the way and that he can bring his people to Fort Laramie where a regular army guard will be posted to protect them. Good Luck, mister! Dismissed!'

Caspar saluted, executed a smart about-face and left.

While Sergeant Hanna attended to getting their horses saddled and the picking out of two spare mounts and saddle rations, Caspar

160

went looking for Jim Bridger.

He found him in a far corner of the stables, sprawled out on some bales of hay in a drunken sleep, a two-thirds empty bottle of whiskey clutched in a dangling left hand.

'Jim! Jim! Wake up!' Caspar said, shaking his shoulder.

'Who—who—lemme 'lone—!' his words slurred. He opened his eyes, focussed them owlishly on Caspar. 'Oh, ishyou, Lieutenant.'

'This is important, Jim. I'm going to try to intercept Chief Black Kettle before he gets to Chief Spotted Tail. If I manage this, do you think he'll listen to me?'

'Listen tuh yo', Black Kettle? Ordinarily he wud, Lieutenant, but them bastids killed his wife. Like they done my Yaller Moon.' He took a stiff drink.

'What about Dull Knife or Little Wolf, would they listen to me?'

'Howlin' mad, both of 'em. Stay clear away, Lieutenant, they'd lif' yore hair quick as scat, thas' jus' exactly whut they'd do.' His voice trailed off. He started to snore.

CHAPTER SEVENTEEN

Sergeant Hanna was already mounted and holding the lead rope of his spare horse when Caspar came out of the stables. A striker held

Caspar's big appaloosa and a second mount, a rangy Morgan.

'What did Jim say about Black Kettle, Lieutenant?' Sergeant Hanna asked, as Caspar swung up into the saddle and took the lead rope of the Morgan from his striker. Caspar merely made a swift handcut across his throat for reply.

'That figgers,' Sergeant Hanna commented grimly.

Troopers from A and B Troops were leading their horses out onto the Parade where already six transport wagons, each drawn by four mules, were waiting. A battery of howitzers cut across the Parade, guns, caissons and hooves kicking up festoons of dust. As Caspar and Sergeant Hanna cantered past the assembling column, Caspar saw Captain Fetterman emerge from Headquarters, drawing on his riding gauntlets. He looked to be in a bad temper. Caspar knew that his father had no choice other than to give Captain Fetterman the command, because Captain Buchanan was away on leave in St. Louis. He hoped his father had given Captain Fetterman explicit orders to avoid provoking a fight. He recalled what Lieutenant George Ransome had told him about the Captain's boast that given fifty troopers he'd ride through the whole Sioux Nation. This time he'd have one hundred and fifty troopers, plus a battery of howitzers. To

162

Caspar, the possibilities of this proving a peaceful patrol were far from encouraging.

When the sun dropped behind Laramie Peak, Caspar and Sergeant Hanna pulled up to change mounts. They had covered some sixty-odd miles at full gallop and both horses the men had been riding were blowing, lathered and sweat-soaked. They had seen no tracks of a big village and travois moving. No sign of advance scouts of the Northern Cheyennes. Caspar gave his big appaloosa a quick rub down, then they switched mounts and were off again at full gallop.

At moonrise, Captain Fetterman halted the column by a stream in a gully below Laramie Peak. He gave the men one hour to water the horses and mules and to eat their supper. He would have liked to have made night camp, but his explicit orders from Major Collins were to proceed as expeditiously as possible to the Platte River Crossing. Secretly he hoped that neither Caspar nor his column would arrive at the Platte River Crossing in time to prevent Black Kettle from carrying the war pipe to Chief Spotted Tail. He wanted the Sioux to hit the war trail. He wanted a chance to crack into them.

The column was about to move out when it was joined by a lone trooper. He wore the uniform of the Colorado Volunteers. He was an Indian. His name was Little Big Man. He rode his mustang up to Captain Fetterman and saluted smartly.

'Me Little Big Man,' he grinned proudly.

'I know that! Sergeant Cotter!'

'Disarm this red bastard. And put him under arrest!'

Sergeant Cotter lunged his horse at Little Big Man, whose hand had flashed to his knife. He caught the Indian's knife wrist in an iron grip. Another trooper ranged his mount alongside Little Big Man, whipped his carbine from the saddleboot and jabbed the muzzle into his side.

'Little Big Man is a Soldier Coat! He is a Soldier Coat! Why do this bad thing to him?' Little Big Man demanded angrily.

'When the Colorado Volunteers massacred the Northern Cheyennes of Chief Black Kettle, Little Big Man showed them the way to attack the village. My orders are to arrest any Colorado Volunteers I find!' Captain Fetterman informed him.

'The Soldier Coat Chief Chivington told Little Big Man to show him the secret way. Little Big Man wears the soldier's coat. He must obey orders!' Little Big Man retorted defiantly.

'Has Little Big Man seen anything of Black Kettle's Cheyennes moving northwest?' Captain Fetterman barked, changing the subject.

'Little Big Man stay away from Cheyennes. They chop him into small pieces.' Little Big

Man shook his head and grinned.

Captain Fetterman stared at him coldly. 'Little Big Man was ordered out of Fort Laramie, why now does he come to me?'

'Pretty quick the Soldier Coats fight the Lakotas. Little Big Man then be big help to the Soldier Coats,' Little Big Man replied, hopefully.

'You might at that,' Captain Fetterman gave his short barking laugh. 'Sergeant, detail two troopers to keep this treacherous bastard under close arrest until we see if we need him.'

About two miles from the Platte River Crossing Caspar and Sergeant Hanna came upon evidence of the migration of the Northern Cheyennes. In the bright moonlight the signs were unmistakable: a wide area of tracks, showing the unshod hoofprints of guarding warriors, and the multiple drag ruts from the many travois, bearing the sick and wounded, food and folded lodges. They had come from the southwest and cut into the Bozeman Road that Caspar and Sergeant Hanna now traveled, a road once open for miners heading for Montana, but long since closed by the Lakotas at the Powder River.

They drew rein and glumly contemplated the tracks.

'From the horse droppings, I'd say they went by six to eight hours ago,' Caspar said. 'If they were Black Kettle's Northern

Cheyennes, we're in trouble, Mike.'

'Course there's nothing says they're Northern Cheyennes, sir. On the other hand, they wouldn't be a Shoshone or Crow war party, not with travois, squaws and dogs along.' He brightened with a thought. 'Could be Red Cloud's Minneconjous too, Lieutenant.'

Caspar shook his head. 'Red Cloud's are camped further west on the Wind River. I'm almost certain it is Black Kettle's Northern Cheyennes. Let's go!'

They left, breaking into full gallop.

On a hill beyond the east bank of the North Platte River a group of coyotes howled dismally, which was in keeping with the desolation of the river bank, where four new death scaffolds were occupied by silent, blanket-wrapped bodies. A fifth dead scaffold neared completion.

At work on the death scaffold was a pretty young squaw. When she finished tying the last crosspiece of peeled willow branch to one of the uprights with rawhide, she gasped and clung weakly to the upright pole. She held one hand against a wide rawhide bandage across her stomach. It was saturated with blood, some old and dried, some fresh and bubbling out. At her feet lay a small baby, wrapped in a torn blanket. Her name was White Deer. She was a Northern Cheyenne.

When she heard Caspar and Sergeant

Hanna splashing across the river shallows, she turned like a wild animal at bay.

Caspar and Sergeant Hanna pulled up close to her.

'Cheyenne,' Caspar said, quietly. He dismounted and tossed his reins to his companion. White Deer whipped out a knife from her belt.

'Watch out, Lieutenant!' Sergeant Hanna warned sharply. 'Them squaws are pure hell at cutting!'

Caspar ignored the warning and walked slowly toward the young woman.

'Soldier Coat!' she spat, her eyes glittered in the moonlight.

Caspar spoke softly. 'My name is Cas. My mother was Pretty Valley, an Oglala-Lakota. You have been hurt. Cas will help you.' He took a step closer, and her knife flashed at him. He caught her wrist, held it firmly but gently and asked, 'When did Chief Black Kettle cross the river?'

'When the sun was in the middle! The Soldier Coats will not catch him again.' The knife fell from her hand, and her head fell forward.

Caspar caught her and lowered her gently to the ground. 'Mike, bring water and bandages!' he snapped.

White Deer's eyes opened slowly, hate appeared then eased away as she saw that Caspar meant her no harm. Mike ran up with a canteen and a roll of bandage.

'Holy mother of God, her belly's been saber slit. How the hell did that poor girl come all this distance,' he breathed.

Caspar shook his head and held the canteen to the girl's lips. She drank only a little. When he started to unwind the rawhide blood-stained bandage from around her middle, she shook her head.

'The shadow of Younkelo even now stands behind White Deer.' She reached weakly for the small bundle wrapped in a torn blanket close by.

'She wants her baby, Mike.'

Mike carefully picked up the small blanket and swore under his breath. 'Take a look at this, Lieutenant.'

Caspar glanced at the baby and his mouth tightened. Its tiny forehead had been smashed by a bullet. Maggots were at work in the gaping wound. He took the small bundle from Sergeant Hanna and White Deer glanced at it. Her eyes clouded over and a sigh escaped her lips. Caspar gently arranged the small bundle in her arms and stood up.

'This death scaffold isn't very strong but it will have to serve. Bring one of my blankets, Mike. We'll wrap them both in it.'

Sergeant Hanna helped Caspar lift the blanket-wrapped bodies of White Deer and her baby onto the platform.

'We'll put their heads at the western end,

Mike, so they can face the sunrise.'

Sergeant Hanna gave him a puzzled look.

'Now bring me some bacon from my saddle bag.'

When Sergeant Hanna returned, Caspar wound some strips of bacon around the top pole near White Deer's head. 'It ought to be pemmican, but this will have to serve for the long journey to Wanagi Yata.' He stepped back, touched the fingers of his left hand to his forehead.

'Lieutenant, do you really believe all that foofaraw?'

'Sometimes I do, Mike. Wanagi Yata is their spirit land, corresponds to the Christians' heaven. My mother believed in it.'

Sergeant Hanna nodded his head thoughtfully. 'Aye, she did at that, Lieutenant, and a proper lady she was, too.'

'Most religions are similar, Mike, they just use different names for the same thing. The Lakotas and the Cheyennes worship Mother Earth and Wi, the sun, and Pte, the buffalo, and the four great directions, north, south, east and west. And, of course, their main god is Wakan Tanka.'

'What about this Younkelo that White Deer said was standing behind her?'

'Younkelo is their god of death.'

'Kinda spooky, isn't it. And who does the Lieutenant worship? I ask that respectfully, sir.'

'Me? Why, Mike, I guess I sort of pray to God, Jesus and Wakan Tanka.' He smiled faintly. 'I like to play it safe. And, believe me, I'm going to be praying to all three that I can find Black Kettle and make him listen to reason.'

Sergeant Hanna was instantly concerned. 'According to White Deer, Black Kettle crossed the North Platte when the sun was in the middle today. That'd be between twelve and one o'clock. He's got eight to nine hours start on you. Chances are he's already smoked the war pipe with Chief Spotted Tail.'

Caspar had walked to his big appaloosa and mounted up. 'Chief Spotted Tail and I understand each other, Mike. I'm counting on him helping me to talk to Black Kettle.'

'Well, Lieutenant,' Mike grinned, 'so long as you're set on riding into that fiery furnace, we may as well get on with it.'

Caspar shook his head. 'Not we, Mike. Just me. You'll stay here as liason to explain what happened to Captain Fetterman.'

'Aw, now, Lieutenant. Old Mike isn't about to let you go busting into the lion's den all by yourself,' Sergeant Hanna expostulated, fully aware that he had overstepped the gulf between enlisted man and officer.

Caspar took no exception to this bridging of the gap. The sergeant was an old friend and, when they were alone he had never pulled rank on him. He said, 'Mike, I appreciate you wanted to come along but the column is commanded by Captain Fetterman, who knows that my orders were to try to reach the Platte River Crossing before Black Kettle. I had no orders to go beyond this point. Off the record, Mike, Captain Fetterman hates my guts—maybe its because I am half Lakota. He'd like nothing better than to hang a courtmartial on me. You stay here! That's an order, old friend! My spare mount is pretty well blown, so I'll just take Lakota.'

He rode off at a gallop, for the broad trail of the Cheyennes was easy to follow in the bright moonlight.

Sergeant Hanna stared after him until he vanished over a rise and his thoughts traveled back to the years when as a private, he had been first posted to the regiment at Fort Laramie in 1850, and where he had drawn duty as orderly to First Lieutenant Rufus Collins. In that capacity, he was thrown much into the company of young Caspar, aged ten. He had taught the boy soldiering and the manual at arms. But riding was unnecessary. Young Caspar spent most of his time away from the post schoolroom in the company of his Lakota friends, Tashunka, He Dog, Lone Bear, and later with Little Singing Stream. He had always enjoyed seeing the youngster ride his pony at full gallop across the Parade,

171

one knee hooked under a Lakota war rope and pretending to shoot arrows from beneath his pony's neck, all the while emitting fierce Lakota war whoops. He knew that the boy's father, then a captain, had frowned on such wild exhibitions, but he had never failed to note the sparkle of pleasure they brought to the dark eyes of his mother, Pretty Valley.

Sergeant Hanna had been at Fort Laramie when the Grattan Massacre occurred and the Lakotas, afraid of Army reprisals, had swiftly vanished in the great vastness of the West. The loss of his Lakota friends had served to cause young Caspar to turn to him and he soon developed an almost parental affection for him.

Being ordered to remain behind while the lieutenant went alone on his dangerous mission made Sergeant Hanna an unhappy man. He cursed Captain Fetterman with deep feeling, then began to try to strengthen the flimsy death scaffold of White Deer and her baby, because that was what he knew the lieutenant would want him to do.

At sunup Sergeant Hanna was still working on the death scaffold when Captain Fetterman forded the river with A Troop in advance of the column.

Captain Fetterman drew rein beside the death scaffold.

'What the flaming hell do you think you're doing, Sergeant?' he demanded arrogantly.

Sergeant Hanna saluted stiffly, his face devoid of expression. 'Just fixing the death scaffold for a young Cheyenne squaw. Her belly'd been saber slit and her baby'd been shot in the head. Courtesy of the Colorado Volunteers, sir.'

'Very touching, but we're not here on burial duty, Sergeant! Where is Lieutenant Collins?'

'Before she died, White Deer, that was the name of the young Cheyenne squaw, sir,' Sergeant Hanna answered woodenly, 'told us Black Kettle had crossed the North Platte about noon yesterday. Lieutenant Collins took off after him. If he can't find Black Kettle, he said he'd find Spotted Tail and try to talk him out of joining in the fight. The lieutenant left me as liason to explain the situation to you, sir.'

'I trust Mr. Collins has an interesting visit with his relatives,' Captain Fetterman said. He cast an amused glance at Lieutenant Ransome and Lieutenant Gourlay of B Troop. Lieutenant Gourlay, a blond, gray-eyed young man of Scottish ancestry, was not amused. Lieutenant Ransome guffawed, both at the quip and also to ingratiate himself further with Captain Fetterman. Sergeant Hanna felt his gorge rise.

He said woodenly, 'May I respectfully suggest that the Captain's last remark was uncalled for?'

Captain Fetterman turned sharply, but managed to retain his sardonic coolness. Sergeant Hanna's stiff posture and expressionless face could not be faulted. Also, he had used the word respectfully. Captain Fetterman studied the man's face for a moment, knowing the latent anger that only an enlisted man knew how to conceal. When he spoke his voice was softly supercilious.

'How long have you been in the Army, Sergeant?'

'Over sixteen years, sir,' came the prompt reply.

'Over sixteen years,' Captain Fetterman appeared to savor the words. Lieutenant Ransome prepared for another of the captain's famous sardonic quips.

'Then, in all those sixteen years, Sergeant,' Captain Fetterman continued, 'surely you must have heard of the word insubordination?'

'Yes, sir. I have. And may I respectfully state that I have also heard of the words "conduct unbecoming to an officer and a gentleman?"'

Captain Fetterman's face darkened. At that moment, Sergeant Hanna saw, past the captain's shoulder, Little Big Man sitting his mustang between troopers Bailey and Hoffman, and he lost his calm. 'May I respectfully ask the Captain what that murdering son of a bitch is doing with the column?' He pointed at the Oglala renegade.

Captain Fetterman was glad the subject had been changed.

He gave his short, barking laugh and said, 'Ah, you must be referring to Little Big Man, Sergeant. Being an officer and a gentleman, I prefer to call him that treacherous bastard! But to answer your question. Little Big Man has been disarmed and is presently under close arrest. When we return to Fort Laramie he'll be tossed into the guardhouse. However, in the interim, should we be fortunate enough to encounter the stinking Sioux, his treacherous talents might prove extremely helpful.' He turned to lieutenants Ransome and Gourlay. 'We'll take a two hour rest, gentlemen. Have the men water the horses and mules and have the cooks serve up a hot breakfast.'

They saluted. Lieutenant Ransome turned his mount to face A Troop. Lieutenant Gourlay cantered down the line for B Troop.

'Prepare to dismount' Lieutenant Ransome ordered.

Sergeant Cotter bellowed, 'Bailey, Hoffman, keep a sharp eye on Little Big Man. If he tries to sneak away, shoot the murdering son of a bitch!' He shot a mischievous grin at his friend Sergeant Hanna.

CHAPTER EIGHTEEN

He Dog lay flat on the crest of a nearby hill, hidden, watching the distant troopers below watering their horses and mules. His face and upper body were painted for war with vermillion and blue streaks and circles. No longer his usual amiable self, his dark eyes were narrow and hate-filled as he made count of the enemy.

Presently, he squirmed backwards until he was below the crest of the hill and ran quickly down the slope to where Lone Bear stood, holding the war ropes of both ponies.

'Many Soldier Coats and four wagon-guns,' he cried. *'Hoppo hoppo up!'*

Both warriors leapt onto their ponies and galloped away, plying their rawhide wrist whips diligently.

At high noon Caspar paused to water his big appaloosa in the north fork of the Powder River. Beyond, the trail left by the fleeing Cheyennes vanished into a pine forest that spread over the lower slopes of the Big Horn Mountains. The broad trail had been an easy one to follow, but for Caspar it had been a grim, pathetic trail. He had passed many hastily constructed death scaffolds and, in most cases, the silent blanket-wrapped occupants had been very small, mute evidence that many of the victims of the massacre had been little children.

Seven miles back Caspar had come upon tracks that had crossed those left by the Cheyennes, tracks that had crossed diagonally. But there had been none made by travois—just those made by several hundred unshod ponies. These could only have been made by a large war party that was heading due north, which would bring it considerably east of the Oglala-Lakota village.

If they had been Crows, Shoshones or Snakes they would have followed the fleeing Cheyennes for ponies and scalps, but no sign showed that they had crossed the trail after the Cheyennes had passed through. So, he reasoned they must have been one of the Lakota tribes, probably Chief Red Cloud's Minneconjous. The big question in his mind was where they were going and why.

Five Indian ponies nuzzled among the pine needles, seeking grass in a small clearing in the forest. Lashed to each pony were the two poles of a travois on which lay a badly wounded victim of the Sand Creek massacre. Tethered under the pines were three more ponies, but these, in contrast to the travel-worn ponies with the travois, were fat and sleek. One was a beautiful pinto.

The hands and forearms of Evening Star, Brown Otter and Deep Waters were blood-stained from attending the wounded.

Their shoulders and breasts glistened with perspiration from working under the hot sun. A wrinkled old Cheyenne, many years past the fighting age, stood watch. He was armed with a feather bedecked lance.

The body of the young Cheyenne warrior that lay on the travois was emaciated and bathed in sweat. His cheeks were sunken and his eyes fever ridden. Blood dribbled from his lips and his breathing was rasping and labored. His young squaw wiped the blood from his lips with a piece of wet rawhide.

Evening Star gently lifted the deermoss poultice to expose the gaping wound in his right chest. Maggots crawled around festering flesh. Blood welled up in the center with each racking breath.

When Brown Otter handed Evening Star a fresh poultice of deermoss she saw the wound. 'Brown Otter would rather be dead than have those bad things inside her,' she gasped.

'The crawling things eat the poisoned flesh and soon the wound will be cleaned,' Evening Star explained. She placed the fresh deermoss poultice over the wound.

A sharp spasm shook the emaciated man's body. He tried to use his hands to push his shoulders up. His squaw pressed them down gently but firmly. A racking cough shook him again, bright blood gushed from his mouth. He collapsed, his head sagged to one side, his mouth slackly open.

Evening Star placed a hand over the man's heart. She held it there for a moment, then said quietly, 'It is done. Finished!'

The young squaw set up a wild keening. She whipped a knife from her belt and slashed her legs in the old Cheyenne sorrow way. Then she pulled her blanket over her head and her wild keening became muffled. Evening Star's eyes filled and she said to Brown Otter, 'Deep Waters and Brown Otter must build a death scaffold. It must be done very quickly.'

She picked up a water container and moved to the next travois. On it lay a young squaw, her deerskin smock was spread over her from neck to knees, to protect her from the sun. Her name was West Wind.

'Is the pain still a big pain?' Evening Star asked solicitiously.

'The pain is not so big. But West Wind is thirsty.'

Evening Star untied the rawhide thong at the neck of the water container, which was made from *Wasna*, the large intestine of the buffalo. She lifted the squaw's head and watched her drink thirstily. 'Too much water will make West Wind sick,' she cautioned.

She threw back the squaw's covering smock to check her wounds. Deermoss poultices covered the wounds where her breasts had been cut off and where she had

179

been crotch scalped. She sprinkled water on the deermoss poultices to keep them damp, then retied the rawhide thong at the water container's neck.

Just as she had recovered the young squaw with her deerskin smock, she heard the sharp danger cry from the old Cheyenne warrior. She saw the old Cheyenne moving as swiftly as his ancient legs would permit toward the back trail, his feathered lance held low for attack. Then she saw Caspar riding slowly through the trees. The next instant she was running like a deer.

Caspar reined his big appaloosa back to avoid the oncoming lance thrust just as Evening Star caught up with the old warrior and threw himself upon him in time to prevent his lance thrust.

'No! No!' she cried. 'It is Cas! The strong friend of the Lakotas!'

The old warrior lowered his lance, but still eyed Caspar with undisguised hatred.

Caspar swung down quickly, looped the reins of Lakota around his arms, then Evening Star was in his arms. The old Cheyenne warrior turned away, muttering to himself.

Caspar kissed her eyes. His hands caressed her full, young breasts and felt their instant response. Her lips clung to his a moment. Then she said, 'This love thing is very strong between Cas and Star.' Suddenly she became filled with anxiety. 'Cas must go back! He must go back now! He must ride very fast!'

'Easy, easy,' Caspar grinned, placing his hand gently over her lips, smothering her torrent of words. 'Black Kettle has not had time to carry the war pipe to the lodges of the Oglala-Lakotas on the Tongue River.'

'Hear me, Cas!' she cried. 'When Star told her father of the big hurting and killing on Sand Creek he rode fast to meet Chief Black Kettle. They have smoked the war pipe together.' Her fear rose. 'So Cas must ride away fast!'

Caspar stiffened. This was bad news. He grasped her upper arms firmly and said, 'Now Star must hear Cas! My father, the Soldier Coat Chief, has sent many wagons filled with blankets, food and medical supplies. He has also sent a white doctor to help the Northern Cheyennes. Star must take Cas very fast to talk to her father and to Chief Black Kettle.'

'Star no longer knows where to find her father and Chief Black Kettle,' she cried breathlessly.

'You mean they are now leading war parties?'

She hesitated, then became frantic. 'Star cannot betray her people! But all Soldier Coats are to be killed. Cas must ride fast. Very fast! He will only be safe beyond the Platte River.'

'Stay away from the fighting!' He kissed

her, mounted Lakota quickly, turned into the back trail and vanished among the pines at a gallop.

Evening Star stared after Caspar's retreating form with growing apprehension, because on the previous night, when she and many Oglala-Lakota girls rode to meet the wounded of the Northern Cheyennes, they had startled a lone white buffalo. To see a white buffalo was an important omen among the Lakotas. Ten years ago she had seen one. Caspar had killed it and he had given the hide to her, and so his image had always remained a picture in her mind. But soon after they had returned to the camp of Conquering Bear, many Soldier Coats had come, saying bad things and shooting wagon-guns. All those Soldier Coats were killed. Her eyes filled, soon they brimmed over, as an icy fear for Caspar gripped her heart.

The column moved along the floor of the valley, flanked by benches that merged into high bluffs. To the northwest, Pumpkin Butte showed through the distant haze.

Captain Fetterman held the column at a walk. He was in no hurry to bring food, blankets and medical supplies to the suffering Northern Cheyennes. He rode in the lead with Lieutenant Ransome. Behind him came Sergeant Hanna and Corporal Muldoon, guidonbearer of A Troop. They were followed by troopers Bailey and Hoffman, with Little Big Man riding between them under guard. Occasionally, Little Big Man's black eyes searched the high bluffs on either side, but his expressionless face gave no clue to his own secret thoughts.

Lieutenant Ransome said, 'I've been thinking, sir.'

'Second Lieutenants aren't supposed to think, mister,' Captain Fetterman laughed.

'I'm serious, sir. If Colonel Chivington had pulled his attack in January or February during the deep snow and bitter cold, he could have caught Black Kettle and his Northern Cheyennes flat-footed and wiped them out.'

'An idea, mister. You may prove to be a military tactician yet. But, we'll have to wait until we get sufficient reenforcements and can hit all the big winter camps at one time, so there'd be no chance for them to send warnings to the other villages. And that miracle, mister, won't happen until we've won the war against the Confederacy.'

'That shouldn't be too far away, sir, after all, we've got the factories, the arms, the food and thousands of fresh troop reserves to bolster our attacks. While the South's practically barefoot and bulletless.'

'A quite logical theory, mister. But you've overlooked one thing.'

'What's that, sir?'

'Those Johnny Rebs have got guts!

Personally, I'd feel safer putting my money on your first tactical theory, mister. In fact, the more I think about it the better I like it.'

CHAPTER NINETEEN

Sergeant Hanna saw movement in the distant, shimmering heat of the trail ahead. He quickly stood up in his stirrups for a better view. Suddenly, he grinned.

'Captain, here comes Lieutenant Collins!' He broke in on the captain's somewhat supercilious dissertation.

All stood in their stirrups, straining their eyes ahead. Someone in uniform was appearing out of the dancing heat waves. There was no mistaking Lieutenant Collins' big appaloosa. He came at full gallop.

Captain Fetterman raised his right arm.

'Column, halt!' he ordered, in the long sing-song of the cavalry. His command was picked up and carried down the column. Sergeant Hanna kicked his mount forward.

'Permission to go meet the lieutenant, Captain?' he requested. 'There might be someone on his tail.'

'Permission not granted, Sergeant!' Captain Fetterman returned without hesitation, his eyes fixed on the distant rider. 'Lieutenant Collins does appear to be in something of a hurry at that,' he commented drily.

'Possibly he found his Cheyenne cousins a trifle short on conversation, sir,' Lieutenant Ransome smirked, as he unscrewed the stopper of his canteen and took a long drink.

'Easy on the water under the full sun, mister,' Captain Fetterman snapped. 'Can bring on sunstroke and sets a bad example for the men!'

'Sorry, sir,' Lieutenant Ransome replied, not in the least chastened by the rebuke. 'The pleasant surprise at finding Lieutenant Collins returning alive caused me to forget your previous lectures, sir,' he grinned confidently.

Amusement tugged at the corners of the captain's thin lips. He always enjoyed Lieutenant Ransome's innuendos when they were directed at the major's half-breed son. The young man had absorbed his own credo with respect to all Indians and it pleased his vanity to have created the image of a knight on a white horse to a junior officer.

Sergeant Hanna bridled his anger. He unscrewed the top of his canteen, took a long swig, swished it around in his mouth, then spat it out, thus taking his own pleasure in cheating the captain out of the quick reprimand he was on the verge of delivering.

'Just demonstrating to the lieutenant how to get rid of the dust, without danger of sunstroke, sir,' he explained innocently.

Captain Fetterman merely nodded. He was fully aware that Sergeant Hanna was resorting to the enlisted man's time-honored method of giving an officer a bad time without laying himself open to a charge of insubordination. But, he promised himself, one day the sergeant would make a mistake, then he'd have the sergeant's stripes.

A slight tug on the reins and Lakota eased down his mad gallop. Another small tug and the big appaloosa slid to a halt near Captain Fetterman, coat foam-flecked and velvety nostrils blowing and fluttering.

Caspar and Captain Fetterman exchanged salutes.

'Second Lieutenant Collins reporting back, sir,' Caspar announced formally. Captain Fetterman smiled sardonically as he pretended to study Caspar's back trail. 'Some of your relations chasing you, Mr. Collins?'

Lieutenant Ransome snickered.

'Not yet, sir,' Caspar replied coolly. 'But I'm sure Mr. Ransome will be amused to hear that as soon as Spotted Tail heard about the Sand Creek massacre he rode out with all his Oglala-Lakota warriors, intercepted Black Kettle on the trail and smoked the war pipe with him. This, as you know, sir means that all hell is about to break loose.'

Captain Fetterman gave him a long, searching look. Then his eyes narrowed. 'Just where did you pick up all this amazing

186

information, mister?'

'Sir, about seven miles this side of the north fork of the Powder River I found the tracks of a large war party, these tracks had crossed the tracks left by the fleeing Northern Cheyennes after the Cheyennes had gone by. These new tracks headed north northeast, somewhere behind those bluffs, sir,' Caspar informed him, matter-of-factly.

'How large did you estimate this war party to be?'

'Several hundred, sir. If it was Red Cloud's Minneconjou-Lakotas, it'd number close to eight hundred.'

'Are you sure they were Red Cloud's Minneconjous?'

'For a large war party to get here this fast they'd have to be nearby. Red Cloud has his lodges on the Wind River—only about thirty-miles southwest of here. And if Red Cloud's hit the warpath, so has Sitting Bull. His Hunkpapa lodges are on the Cheyenne River about forty miles northwest on the lower slopes of the Black Hills.' Caspar paused, then added, 'As I said before, sir, it looks like all hell's about to break loose.'

Captain Fetterman uttered his short, barking laugh. 'If your assumption is true, things should stop being so dull pretty quick. But, mister, it's all predicated upon Spotted Tail having actually smoked the war pipe with Black Kettle. You weren't there, so how do you know it happened?'

'I crossed the north fork of the Powder River and found some Lakota girls attending wounded Northern Cheyennes. One of them was Evening Star. She told me her father had smoked the war pipe with Black Kettle, sir.'

'Aaah, now we're getting somewhere, mister,' Captain Fetterman said. 'And did she also tell you about Red Cloud and Sitting Bull?'

'No, sir. That part was my own assumption. Evening Star told me just two things. First, that her father had smoked the war pipe with Black Kettle. The second, and she was very emphatic about this, sir, she begged me to ride away very fast and not to stop until I'd crossed the Platte River. Because only there would I be safe. She wasn't trying to betray her people. She merely preferred having a live husband to a dead one.'

'That makes sense, mister.' Captain Fetterman frowned thoughtfully, then said, 'Didn't you ask her to take you to her father and Black Kettle to tell them about the food, blankets and medicine we're bringing to the Northern Cheyennes?'

'I did, sir, but she told me she didn't know where to find either her father or Black Kettle. To me that meant only one thing—they'd hit the war trail.'

'If it wasn't for the transport wagons, we'd

188

go looking for the Sioux!' Captain Fetterman grated in disappointment.

'I don't know how many Cheyenne warriors Black Kettle's got left, but the Oglalas, Minneconjous and Hunkpapas together can put over two thousand warriors in the field,' Caspar informed him.

'Humph!' Captain Fetterman snorted. 'Sergeant Cotter, bring Little Big Man forward!'

Caspar's head came up sharply. 'Little Big Man?' he snapped incredulously.

'That right, mister,' Captain Fetterman said, amused at Caspar's obvious anger. 'He rode into the column and I had the bastard disarmed and placed under close arrest.'

Little Big Man rode up between his two guards and under the watchful eyes of Sergeant Cotter. The man's black eyes were sullen and suspicious.

Captain Fetterman said sternly, 'Little Big Man has ridden with my Soldier Coats for many hours. Did his eyes see any Lakota or Cheyenne warriors up on the bluffs?'

'The eyes of Little Big Man can see nothing until it is given a proper soldier coat like Big Mouth wears,' he answered.

'He's bucking for Corporal Big Mouth's job, sir,' Lieutenant Ransome laughed.

'I was going to give you a chance to prove you were trustworthy,' Captain Fetterman said. 'Now I wouldn't trust you further than I

189

could throw a buffalo.'

'Little Big Man make good Soldier Coat scout!' The Lakota broke out vehemently. 'Cas is the one not to trust! His heart is strong for Evening Star, for Crazy Horse and for the Lakotas! Stronger than for the Soldier Coats!'

'Sergeant Cotter, take this noisy bastard away!'

'Prisoner and escort, about-face! Forward march!' Sergeant Cotter snapped.

'Sergeant Hanna, my compliments to lieutenants Gourlay and Mason and ask them to join me on the double.'

As the sergeant cantered back down the column, Captain Fetterman lit a cigar and scanned the nearby bluffs and gullys.

'I see no sign of any hostiles, Mr. Collins,' he remarked.

'About the only time you'll see a hostile is when he wants you to see him, sir,' Caspar replied, his eyes searching the high bluffs.

The captain exhaled a cloud of blue smoke. 'I think your love for the Lakotas causes you to endow them with qualities they don't possess, mister,' he commented thinly.

Caspar pointed to a section of high bluff and said, 'If the Captain will look atop that high bluff over there, he'll see mirrors flashing. The Lakotas have their squaws get them from the white traders, then use them for signalling.' He glanced at the high bluffs on the opposite side of the valley and suddenly pointed. 'There's an answering flash. I respectfully suggest that they are endowed with certain qualities, sir.'

'Touche, mister,' he grinned coldly at Caspar. Lieutenants Gourlay and Mason galloped up and saluted.

'Gentlemen,' Captain Fetterman began, 'our mission was to prevent Black Kettle from carrying the war pipe to Spotted Tail. Mr. Collins informs me that such a meeting has occurred and that the Lakotas, or the Sioux as we call them, and the Northern Cheyennes are out for a fight. Now, because we must protect the transport wagons and your battery of howitzers, Lieutenant Mason, we cannot function as mobile attack cavalry. Consequently, for the time being, we must go over to the defense. I propose to take up defense positions on the east bank of the North Platte River and force the Sioux and Cheyennes to come to us.' He paused, and touched a fresh match to his cigar.

Caspar said, 'Sir, if that happens, there's a chance the mission may still be successful.'

'Oh, how do you figure that miracle, mister.'

'With the Platte in flood, they'd have to attack through the shallows at the Platte River Crossing, sir. I could meet Spotted Tail under a flag of truce on the west bank and I think I could get him to make Black Kettle listen to what we want to do for his people. It could possibly settle things without a fight, sir.'

'Possibly, mister, possibly,' Captain Fetterman admitted dubiously. 'If it doesn't work, Lieutenant Mason will let go with his howitzers and blow the Sioux and Cheyennes out of their stinkin' moccasins. A Troop will lead the column, B Troop will act as rear guard. Both troops will put out flankers on both sides of the valley. Mr. Collins, is your horse blown after your Paul Revere ride?'

'No, sir, Lakota still has plenty of bottom.'

'Good,' Captain Fetterman ejaculated. 'I want you to scout ahead of the column and keep a sharp lookout for an ambush. I wanted Corporal Big Mouth and some of his scouts along, but Major Collins felt that with them leading we'd look too much like an armed reconnaisance in force rather than a peace mission. Take Sergeant Hanna with you! We'll back trail out of here now, and we'll go as fast as the transport wagons will permit. Gentlemen, return to your posts!'

The column moved westward along the valley floor at a fast trot, wagons, caissons and guns bouncing and swaying over the rough ground. On either side, the flanking troopers kept pace with the column, alert and watchful for a sudden sortie of hostiles from the side gullys.

High up on the bluffs, the flash of a mirror was picked up and relayed on ahead, crisscrossing the valley below.

Caspar and Sergeant Hanna traveled at an easy lope a half mile in advance of the column, a pace they had maintained for the past two hours so each had time to scout side gullys and still stay well ahead of the column.

A wide outcropping of black volcanic rock crossed the valley floor, and the trail narrowed, causing Caspar and Sergeant Hanna to converge together to get through.

Sergeant Hanna stood up in his stirrups, checking the immediate terrain. 'Thought sure'n hell they'd hit us here, Lieutenant,' he said, shaking his head, puzzled. 'Plenty of good solid rock cover to shoot from and the column pinched into a narrow trail. The opportunity of a lifetime and the Lakotas passed it up. Maybe the captain was right and we've been overrating their fighting abilities, Lieutenant.'

'You're wrong, Mike. If anything, we've been underestimating. First, the Lakotas don't like to fight on foot, and these volcanic rocks'll cut the hell out of the horses hooves, shod or unshod. Next, and I think this accounts for all the mirror signalling, they've spotted our battery of howitzers. A shell bursting here would not only spread shrapnel around but chunks of volcanic rock as well.'

'My respects to the Lakotas,' Sergeant Hanna said. He removed his campaign hat and wiped the sweat from his forehead with the cuff of his gauntlet. 'Cheerist, it's hot! And come sundown the goddamn mosquitoes'll move in. We ought to let the Lakotas keep this whole territory. Belongs to them anyway. Where does the Lieutenant figure they'll hit us?'

Caspar considered a moment, then said, 'About four miles further on you get your first glimpse of the North Platte River. From there on down to the river the bluffs close in and they're shot with gullys. If I were Spotted Tail I'd set up my ambush somewhere in that area. Any better ideas, Mike?'

'If I did, I'd just plain scare myself to death, Lieutenant,' Mike grinned, then added meaningfully, 'Especially with Captain 'Hell-for-leather' Fetterman in command. If we get safely across the Platte, I'll say five Hail Marys and even welcome the goddamn mosquitoes.'

'I'll be with you on the Hail Marys, Mike, and toss in a few *Woyuonihans* to Wakan Tanka, the Lakota supreme god, for good measure.'

CHAPTER TWENTY

Despite the heat and the rivulets of sweat running down inside his heavy woolen tunic, Captain Fetterman felt a rising inner elation at the prospects of getting into a fight with the Sioux and Cheyennes. That his own force would probably be greatly outnumbered bothered him not at all, for he held an unrealistic contempt for the fighting abilities of all races other than white. At that moment, the only cloud on the doughty captain's horizon consisted of his responsibility to protect the gun battery and the transport wagons, and he could not take the opportunity to ride hell for leather through the whole Sioux Nation. However, he consoled himself, even though forced to fight a defensive action, he had the firepower to inflict heavy casualties upon any and all attackers.

Lieutenant Ransome interrupted his pleasant musings with an unorthodox question. He said, 'Sir, unofficially, don't you think it risky to trust Mr. Collins to be advance scout for the column?'

'Just exactly what are you driving at, mister?' Captain Fetterman rejoined noncommittedly.

'Well, sir, you heard Little Big Man's tirade against Mr. Collins, that his heart was not with the Soldier Coats but with the Lakotas and particularly, with Evening Star. As you saw at the fort, sir, she is a raving beauty and,' he grinned lecherously, 'at Spotted Tail's camp, she wore nothing but a loincloth and moccasins. She had the most gorgeous pair of breasts I've ever seen. They could turn a man's head dizzy, sir.'

A sardonic smile touched the corners of Captain Fetterman's mouth. He said, 'Including yourself, I take it, mister?'

'Not my head, sir. My intentions would be strictly dishonorable. I'd merely want to borrow them, not marry them.'

Captain Fetterman uttered his short, barking laugh.

'A forthright answer, by God! But, to reply to your question, mister, it's strictly against regulations to discuss the qualities of one officer with a junior officer. However, I will say this, Mr. Collins graduated from the West Point Military Academy. He took the oath to serve his country and his flag. He is also an officer and a gentleman by act of Congress, and, while he may be inordinately partial to the stinking Indians, I do not believe he would do anything to betray his regiment. Of course, if I found an officer to be reluctant to fire on his red relations, I'd see he drew a courtmartial.'

When they rounded a bend in the narrowing valley, Caspar and Sergeant Hanna caught a glint of the afternoon sun in the distance on the shallow crossing of the North Platte River and pulled up. Each scanned the gullys and bluffs on both sides of the valley carefully.

'See anything, Lieutenant?' Sergeant

Hanna murmured.

'No, Mike. Not yet. But if the Lakotas and the Cheyennes are here, and I think they are, they'll wait until the column comes up. Then they'll spring their trap!'

When the column caught up with Caspar and Sergeant Hanna, Captain Fetterman gave Caspar a questioning look and said, 'You should be almost to the river, Mr. Collins. What held you up?'

Caspar gestured with a hand raised toward the river. 'The valley narrows from here to the river. The bluffs on both sides are shot with gullys. I have a strong hunch that those gullys are hiding from two to three thousand Lakota and Cheyenne warriors. I think we're riding into an ambush, sir.'

Captain Fetterman flipped open the leather case of his binoculars and quickly scanned both sides of the valley toward the river.

Presently, he lowered his binoculars. He gave Caspar a searching look. 'Not one warbonnet, not one feather, not a sign of one stinking redskin. Have you seen any, mister?'

'No, sir. All I've seen were the mirror signals. But I still have a strong hunch we're riding into an ambush, possibly into a trap.'

Lieutenant Ransome sniggered. Captain Fetterman enjoyed his wit being appreciated, so he said, facetiously, 'Well, now, Mr. Collins, based upon this alleged, and I quote, strong hunch, what military tactics would you advise?'

Caspar would have liked nothing better than to slam his fist into that supercilious face but he refused to be baited.

He said evenly, 'Sir, if I were in command, and if the lives of my men were my first consideration, I'd do one of two things. I'd either fall back about three miles to where the valley is wide enough that the Indians could not fire their arrows from the protection of the gullys but would have to ride out into the open and thus come under fire, or I'd take the column at full gallop and try to break through to the river.'

'You would, would you? Well, for your information, mister, I never retreat! Further, the terrain between here and the river is extremely rough. At full gallop all the transport wagons would be wrecked!'

'I meant to add, sir,' Caspar said, unruffled, 'I'd unhitch the mules and abandon the wagons. Many of the Indians would be busy plundering the wagons so I'd have fewer to fight through to make the river.'

'What? Abandon the transport wagons to those red devils? You must be out of your mind, mister!' the captain snorted.

Little Big Man let go a series of wild, wolf howls.

'What the goddamn hell's that lunatic think he's doing?' Captain Fetterman roared.

'It's the Lakota warning of heavy attack! And there they are, sir. Clear across the back trail!' Caspar explained quickly.

A quarter mile behind the column and out of rifle range, mounted warriors spewed from either side of the valley. They dashed out at full gallop, putting on a magnificent exhibition of horsemanship, brandishing guns, feathered lances and bows.

Caspar twisted in the saddle quickly and glanced toward the river.

'Captain,' he cried sharply. 'Look toward the river! They've got us boxed in. It's a trap!'

'By God, they're going to get a fight!' Captain Fetterman exclaimed with rising excitement. 'Battery, forward, at the gallop!' he bellowed.

Out of rifle shot, toward the distant river, hundreds of Lakotas and Cheyennes raced their war ponies out of the side gullys, blocking the way to the river.

'Lieutenant,' Mike said, as he surveyed the growing number of Indians, 'I think I'll say a couple of those Hail Marys right now!'

'You do that, Mike,' Caspar nodded, then saw something that made him wheel his big appaloosa over to where Captain Fetterman held a hurried conference with his other officers. Lieutenant Mason arrived at a gallop with his battery of four howitzers. 'Unlimber, Lieutenant!' Captain Fetterman ordered.

While the artillerymen unlimbered their guns, Caspar ranged his mount alongside Captain Fetterman.

'Sir,' he said, 'may I borrow your binoculars? It's important, sir.'

Captain Fetterman hesitated, then lifted the strap over his head and handed Caspar his binoculars. 'Looking for relatives, mister?'

'No, sir, for a possible way to save lives.'

He focused the binoculars on a large group of Indians who sat their mounts on a slight rise. He said as he studied the group, 'That large group of Indians on the rise to the left, sir. Among them are Crazy Horse, an old friend, and three warbonneted chiefs. One is a Cheyenne, probably Black Kettle, the other two are Lakotas, Red Cloud and Spotted Tail, Chief Spotted Tail.'

Captain Fetterman's triumphant shout interrupted him.

'Lieutenant Mason, that bunch of Indians on that rise to the left! I want a shell dropped right on top of them!'

'I'll lay the gun myself, sir!' Lieutenant Mason snapped. He dismounted quickly and ran to the nearest gun.

Caspar said angrily, 'No, sir. You can't do that! Chief Spotted Tail agreed to always talk with me before making a fight. Goddamn it to hell! Can't you see there's a chance I can get him to call off this fight? Might even get Black Kettle to take the supplies we've

200

brought? I request permission to go talk to Chief Spotted Tail, sir!'

'What?' Captain Fetterman roared, equally angry. 'You expect me to miss a God-given chance to blow Spotted Tail, Red Cloud and Black Kettle out of their dirty moccasins? Permission denied, mister!'

Caspar flipped the binoculars back to Captain Fetterman and yelled, 'You're not only a bastard, you're a fanatic!'

He turned his mount away, kicked it into a gallop. As he went past Corporal Muldoon, guidonbearer of A Troop, he snapped, 'I'll take that, Corporal,' and snatched the guidon from the startled corporal's hand and rode full tilt towards the distant war chiefs.

'Fire when ready!' Captain Fetterman snapped to Lieutenant Mason, who was sighting the howitzer as one of the gunners rammed home a shell.

Sergeant Hanna whipped his carbine from the saddleboot, cocked it and held it on Lieutenant Mason.

'I'll shoot the first son of a bitch who pulls that lanyard!' he threatened.

'Sergeant Cotter, arrest that man!' Captain Fetterman roared.

'Arrest Sergeant Hanna, sir?' Sergeant Cotter spluttered. 'But—but—'

'He's just won himself a courtmartial!'

'At which time, sir,' Sergeant Hanna reminded him wickedly, 'I'll be under oath to report to Major Collins that you ordered Lieutenant Mason to fire on his son!'

'Hold your fire, Lieutenant!' Captain Fetterman swallowed his anger. 'You'll stand courtmartial when we return to Fort Laramie, Sergeant! You and Mr. Collins!'

'If we all return to Fort Laramie, sir, it'll be because of Lieutenant Collins, sir!'

'*Hoye!*' Little Big Man cried. 'The heart of Cas is strong for the Lakotas. He will warn Chief Spotted Tail not to make big target for wagon guns!'

Sergeant Hanna heeled his mount beside Little Big Man. 'Shut that big, ugly mouth or I'll shut it for you!' he gritted.

CHAPTER TWENTY-ONE

Five Cheyennes rode howling out of a side gully to intercept the crazy Soldier Coat who was riding straight for the great war chiefs armed with a Little Soldier Flag.

Caspar saw his danger and leaned low in the saddle, urging Lakota on to greater speed.

Though he felt the big appaloosa respond, he knew that the five Cheyennes would intercept him. Even if he were successful in defending himself with his revolver, he knew that such action would all but kill any chances he might have of getting Spotted Tail and

Black Kettle to listen to reason.

Then help came from an unexpected quarter. Three warriors came off the hill where the great war chiefs sat their horses. They came at full gallop, rifles raised horizontally above their heads, howling their Lakota war cries, warning the Cheyennes to stay away, that this Soldier Coat belonged to them. Leading the trio was Crazy Horse, his face painted with blue streaks of lightning, his body with hail stones. Behind him rode He Dog and Lone Bear.

The five charging Cheyennes pulled back on their rope bridles, angry to be cheated of such an easy prey, but, as the Cheyenne warriors were far less in numbers to the Lakotas, they were in no position to start an intertribal war. The war ponies of the three Lakotas were pulled to a rearing halt as Caspar met them.

'Cas brings big words to Chief Spotted Tail!' Caspar said sharply.

'The blood of the Lakotas and Cheyennes is very hot against the Soldier Coats. The ears of Spotted Tail and Black Kettle may be closed against the words of Cas,' Crazy Horse warned.

'*Hoppo-up!*' Caspar shouted. He spurred Lakota toward the hill. Crazy Horse, He Dog and Lone Bear formed his escort. Crazy Horse on his big buckskin took the lead. Lone Bear and He Dog rode protection on either side of Caspar.

There was no warmth in the painted faces of chiefs Spotted Tail, Red Cloud and Black Kettle as they watched Caspar approach with Crazy Horse, He Dog and Lone Bear. Gray Wolf, the Cheyenne guest of Spotted Tail, had only killing hatred in his black eyes. The close to thirty Lakota warriors in the group watched Caspar with a curiosity that was mingled with suspicion.

Spotted Tail commented gravely to Black Kettle and Red Cloud, 'This young Soldier Coat is called Cas. His mother was Pretty Valley, the daughter of Iron Hand. Until this day his heart has always been good toward the Lakotas. We will hear his words.'

Caspar, Crazy Horse, He Dog and Lone Bear pulled up before the great war chiefs. Caspar inclined his head, touched the tips of the fingers of his left hand to his forehead to Chief Spotted Tail. He said, '*Woyuonihan*! Chief Spotted Tail told Cas that when a bad thing happened between Indians and whites, he and Cas would talk, and the bad thing would walk away. Were the words of Chief Spotted Tail without meaning?'

Spotted Tail said, 'Those words were true words, meant for small misunderstandings.' His voice rose with anger. 'But now many of our Cheyenne cousins lie dead on Sand Creek. Many have come to the Lakotas badly hurt, even women and children!'

204

Gray Wolf nudged his war pony forward. His words were vicious. 'The ears of the Northern Cheyennes are closed to the split-tongued words of any Soldier Coat.'

A quick hand signal from Black Kettle silenced him.

Spotted Tail said coldly, 'The ears of Spotted Tail are open.'

'Hear me well because my words are true words,' Caspar said firmly. 'The Soldier Coats who did this bad thing at Sand Creek were not real Soldier Coats! They were evil white men who only sometimes put on soldier uniforms!'

'At the Soldier Fort Laramie, Crazy Horse heard Big Throat say that this was true, that the Soldier Coat Chief who did this bad thing was called Chivington!' Crazy Horse added his voice to back up Caspar.

'The real Soldier Coats have caught this Chivington. He is now in prison in Fort Lyon. He will be punished! Down there,' Caspar pointed to halted columns, 'are six big wagons filled with food, with molasses, with tobacco, with warm blankets, with bandages and medicine for the Northern Cheyennes. There is also a white-man doctor to care for their sick and their wounded. Soon a new father-agent will come to talk to Chief Black Kettle to ask what more must be done to make the hearts of his people feel good again.'

'The words of this Soldier Coat are lies!'

Gray Wolf spat.

Black Kettle made another vicious hand signal to Gray Wolf, whose hands gripped the rifle across his lap in suppressed fury until the knuckles showed bone-white.

Black Kettle gave Caspar a long, searching look, then he turned to Spotted Tail and said, 'Black Kettle wishes to hold off the attack on the Soldier Coats.'

Spotted Tail nodded, raised a small mirror and sent a series of flashes across and down the valley. In moments, the fierce howling of the warriors died away.

Black Kettle turned once again to Caspar and said, 'The eyes of Black Kettle would like to see what the six big wagons have brought for his people.'

At this Gray Wolf's anger burst out of control. He pointed vigorously with his rifle and raged, 'But the eyes of Gray Wolf see only four wagon-guns! Four wagon-guns that are now pointed at our hearts!'

When Gray Wolf screamed the words wagon-guns, Spotted Tail's head came up sharply. He glanced quickly at the column in the valley. He exclaimed sharply, 'We make a big target! Spread out! *Hoppo-up* away, fast!' He accompanied his order with fast hand signals.

Inwardly, Caspar cursed Captain Fetterman for his insistence on bringing along a battery of howitzers. He said quickly, 'The

206

wagon-guns will not shoot unless the Soldier Coats are attacked!'

Already the clustered warriors were moving away on all sides.

On the valley floor there was a gunflash. Black smoke spewed out. The sound of the gunslam echoed against the bluffs, followed by the scream of an approaching shell. Then it exploded with a thunderclap, fifty feet short of the great war chiefs. Shrapnel flew, horses plunged, and two of the departing warriors were hit.

Gray Wolf's reaction was instantaneous. He cocked his rifle and fired. The heavy bullet slammed into Caspar's chest at point blank range. It tore through his heart. It knocked him off his big appaloosa, and he was dead when his body hit the ground, his right hand still clutching the guidon of A Troop.

With a howl of rage Crazy Horse jumped his buckskin at Gray Wolf. His war club crashed down on Gray Wolf's head, splitting the skull. Blood and gray brain membrane gushed out as he toppled to the ground.

Crazy Horse dismounted, retaining the war rope in his left hand to steady his plunging buckskin. His right hand touched Caspar's face, then felt the jugular in his neck. There was no pulse beat. He lifted his grief-stricken face to Spotted Tail. His voice was bitter, harsh. 'The words of Cas were true words. The Soldier Chief Fetterman down there hated the Lakotas. He hated Cas. Cas was my friend! Now the heart of Crazy Horse is in the ground! This is not a good day for Crazy Horse to fight.'

He gently pried the troop guidon staff from Caspar's dead fingers and wedged it beneath the war rope of his buckskin. He lifted Caspar's body across his saddle blanket and vaulted up behind, taking Caspar's body in his arms. He turned his buckskin over the crest of the rise and away from the fighting.

He rode slowly and heard the explosions of a second, a third and a fourth shell. He felt the concussions, but was filled with the memory of the dream of his father, Worm, the holy man. He recalled how frightened Evening Star had been when he told her and Cas about it. He remembered how certain she had been that Wana Tanka would never allow such a bad thing to come true. Yet that dream had now become a reality. He was riding away from a fight, carrying the body of a Soldier Coat, a Soldier Coat whose name was Cas.

CHAPTER TWENTY-TWO

Captain Fetterman had followed the progress of Caspar through his binoculars. He saw his almost certain death at the hands of the five

Cheyenne warriors and his timely rescue by three Lakotas.

'Mr. Collins came within a hair of missing out on his courtmartial,' he commented.

'Could also be out of the frying pan into the fire, too, sir,' Lieutenant Ransome said smugly.

'That's where you're wrong, Lieutenant,' Sergeant Hanna cut in. 'Those three Lakotas are Crazy Horse, He Dog, and Lone Bear, all old friends of Lieutenant Collins.'

'My compliments on your good eyesight, Sergeant,' Lieutenant Ransome remarked facetiously.

Captain Fetterman, his eyes still glued to his binoculars, said, 'Well, I'll be damned! Mr. Collins is now talking to the war chiefs.'

'Captain, sir, I'll bet a year's pay he talks Black Kettle into calling off the war and accepting those six wagon loads of supplies!' Sergeant Hanna boasted.

Captain Fetterman did not share his enthusiasm.

'And cheating me out of the best target I'll ever get, goddamn it!'

Sergeant Hanna could see that Little Big Man was just waiting for an opportunity to say something that might ingratiate him with Captain Fetterman and gain him a real Soldier Coat. If he opened his big mouth he intended to be close enough to the son of a bitch to shut it.

He casually dismounted and pretended to adjust his saddle girth. He eased his horse closer to where Little Big Man sat between his two guards.

A series of quick mirror flashes glinted from the rise where Caspar was talking with the war chiefs. The howling cries of the Indians died away and an eerie silence followed, broken only by the stomping and snorting of horses.

'Now what the goddamn hell d'you suppose that signal meant?' Captain Fetterman snapped irritably.

'I'd guess that Lieutenant Collins had just talked Spotted Tail into calling off the war, Captain, sir,' Sergeant Hanna offered.

'I don't want guesses, Sergeant! I want an interpretation of those mirror signals from Little Big Man!'

Sergeant Hanna doubled his fist menacingly, but Little Big Man had no intention of missing his golden opportunity. He said, 'Mirror signals mean Chief Spotted Tail has changed plan of attack. Look, see, Cas has warned him about the wagon-guns. Now the big target will pretty quick be small target!'

This last was a shriek as Sergeant Hanna yanked him down from his horse and crashed his big fist into his mouth, knocking him to the ground. Little Big Man's hand fastened on a rock and he leapt at Sergeant Hanna.

The toe of the Sergeant's heaving cavalry boot caught Little Big Man in the crotch and he fell back howling, clutching his groin.

Captain Fetterman barked, 'By God, he's right! *Fire!*' Lieutenant Mason personally yanked hard on the lanyard and his number-one gun fired.

When the black smoke cleared away, fresh mirror flashes blinked from the distant hill amid the smoke of the bursting shell and plunging horses. The howling of the Indians erupted on all sides again.

'You may as well have murdered Lieutenant Collins, you blasted lunatic!' Sergeant Hanna roared at Captain Fetterman.

'That's enough out of you, Sergeant!' Captain Fetterman shouted. 'Now get that Indian back on his horse and mount up yourself! Sergeant Trotter!'

'Sir?'

'I want the wagon drivers to unhitch the mules and bring them forward. Bring Dr. Lunt with you, too. I'm abandoning the wagons. With the Sioux busy looting them, it will keep them off our rear!'

Sergeant Trotter saluted and galloped back down the column.

'Lieutenant Mason!'

'Sir?'

Captain Fetterman remained cool in the crisis. His orders came crisp and decisive. 'I want four rounds of canister laid right smack among those stinking Sioux blockading our passage to the river. Then you'll limber up fast. A Troop will cut a path for your battery to the river! You'll cross the river and unlimber on the bluffs and immediately open a covering barrage while the rest of the column crosses over! Snap to it, Lieutenant!'

The gun crews moved swiftly to Lieutenant Mason's orders. Powder charges and shell were rammed home. Captain Fetterman walked his mount over to where A Troop sat their horses in column of two's, waiting. He called out forcefully, 'Keep a tight rein on your mounts when the guns fire. Then we'll charge. When in shooting distance of the Sioux, fire your carbines, then slam them into your saddleboots and draw sabers. We'll cut our way through to the river!'

His eyes searched the hundreds of Sioux and Cheyenne warming up their war ponies on the valley floor some four hundred yards ahead.

'Battery ready to fire, sir!' Lieutenant Mason sang out.

'Fire!' Captain Fetterman ordered.

All four guns let go at once. Black smoke belched out, the ground shook to the explosions and gun recoil.

Through the black smoke, A Troop erupted at a canter, Captain Fetterman and Lieutenant Ransome in the lead.

'Column of four's, gallop!' came the run of

command. Even files joined up with odd files as the troop thundered toward the enemy, many of whom were down or scattered by the shellfire.

Sergeant Hanna rode behind the two officers, revolver in hand, trying to blank his mind to what he felt sure had been the murder of Lieutenant Collins. Trying to forget his raging hatred against Captain Fetterman, one thing he had to give the bastard, he was leading the attack. He had guts!

The Sioux and Cheyennes raced out of side gullys as carbines rattled. Then the rasp of sabers drawn and the head of the column slammed into a double line of Sioux. Sabers slashed wickedly. Arrows thrummed. Many troopers were hit. Some toppled from their saddles.

Lieutenant Ransome took the feathered lance of a warbonneted chief through his chest and went down. Sergeant Hanna caught the chief with two bullets from his revolver.

Sergeant Hanna slashed his saber down on the naked shoulder of a Cheyenne, then the warrior's mate drove an arrow through the sergeant's neck, severing his jugular. Sergeant Michael Hanna never finished saying his five Hail Marys.

On Captain Fetterman's order, at the river bank, A Troop divided and wheeled to face the enemy. Carbines were hastily reloaded.

Many of the men were wounded. Several riderless horses came up and took their accustomed places in formation.

Through the gap, Lieutenant Mason's guns came at full gallop, followed by B Troop. A Troop fired a volley into the howling mass of Lakotas and Cheyennes, then hit the river.

As soon as B Troop gained the eastern bank, the men dismounted and poured a covering fire into the Indians, who were pursuing the shattered remains of A Troop into the river. The concentrated covering fire knocked down many of the pursuers and drove the others back.

When more and more Lakotas and Cheyennes came howling toward the river, Lieutenant Mason's howitzers went into action, forcing them to scatter for cover.

Captain Fetterman sent a dispatch to Major Rufus Collins at Fort Laramie. He reported a heavy running fight with a vastly superior force of Lakotas and Northern Cheyennes at the Platte River Crossing. He requested reenforcements, ammunition, food and medical supplies, as many of his men were wounded. In his dispatch, Captain Fetterman made no mention of Second Lieutenant Caspar Collins.

CHAPTER TWENTY-THREE

The after glow of the setting sun flamed the sky above Pa Sapa, the sacred Black Hills of the Lakotas, touching with fire the edge of the black thunder clouds moving in from the east. The fighting was over. Lightning flashed and thunder rolled in the distance. The evening breeze freshened by the advancing storm coughed through the pines and down the gullys.

The death scaffold was newly built. The four upright poles were thick and sturdy, the crosspieces and platform were lashed firmly in place with tough, rawhide thongs.

The quiet form that lay on the platform was wrapped in a red blanket. Tied to an upright pole near the head was Caspar's campaign hat and his saber, together with a *wasna* filled with pemmican for the long journey to Wanagi Yata, land of the Great Spirit. At Caspar's feet, the guidon of A Troop was lashed to an upright pole, its forked flag riffled by the evening breeze.

Evening Star gently urged her pinto pony alongside the death scaffold. She wore the white buffalo robe over her shoulders and head that Caspar had given her many years ago on the Shell River. Blood trickled down her shapely legs from the ceremonial knife

215

cuts of mourning for the dead. She placed her hands on the scaffold platform and stood up on her saddle blanket. Slowly, ceremoniously, she removed the sacred white buffalo robe from her shoulders and carefully spread it over the silent, red-blanketed figure.

Her eyes filled, brimmed over, spilling down her cheeks and onto her bare breasts. She placed both hands over her left breast, then slowly opened them toward Caspar's body, like a flower to the warmth of the rising sun.

Nearby, Crazy Horse stood, holding his buckskin by its rope bridle, watching Evening Star. His lightning streaked war paint had been removed, his eyes were steady, enigmatical, masking his inner turmoil at seeing Evening Star symbolically giving her heart to Caspar to take with him on the long journey to Wanagi Yata, which also meant that she would never marry, but would become a holy woman, devoting her life to caring for the helpless ones, the old, the sick and the little children.

Evening Star inclined her head, touched the tips of the fingers of her left hand to her forehead, then dropped down into her saddle blanket and slowly rode away.

Crazy Horse moved to the death scaffold, leading his buckskin. For a long moment his eyes traveled over the silent form of his boyhood friend and upon the fluttering guidon of A Troop. He took a deep breath and his words came both grief-stricken and resonant.

'Hear me, Cas, though your voice cannot answer. This death scaffold is strong, so none can break this peace that Cas has found. Not even the winds from the four great directions that whisper through the Little Soldier Flag that held your heart. Wait for me in Wanagi Yata, my only Soldier Coat friend!'

He bowed his head, touched the fingertips of the left hand to his forehead, paused, then vaulted onto his buckskin and rode slowly away, away to fulfill a destiny that would see him become the foremost of the great Lakota war chiefs, only to fall victim of treacherous assassination at the hands of an Indian Reservation policeman, an Oglala-Lakota policeman who wore a Soldier Coat, Little Big Man.

The rising wind whipped out the little red and white forked guidon of A Troop, making visible its markings. From high in the Sacred Black Hills to join in the sough of the rising wind came the lonely howl of a timber wolf.

Photoset, printed and bound in Great Britain by REDWOOD PRESS LIMITED, Melksham, Wiltshire